JACK LONDON is best known for his books *The Call of the Wild*, *White Fang*, and *The Sea-Wolf*, but he was an incredibly prolific writer who left behind more than fifty volumes of novels, stories, journalism, and essays, many of which are still read around the world. Born in San Francisco in 1876 and named John, he adopted the name Jack during an adolescence spent working various hard-labor jobs, and later decided to become a writer in order to escape the fate of life as a factory worker. A summer spent in the Yukon in his twenties provided ample material to launch a career that would see him manipulate the media and embrace the writer persona as few before him had. The first full-length feature film made in America was based on *The Sea-Wolf*, and London would live to see several of his works adapted for the big screen.

A committed if conflicted socialist, he possessed a strong desire for capitalist success (he endorsed commercial products in advertisements), but would use the platform his fame afforded him to endorse socialism, women's suffrage, and prohibition, and to break the taboo of leprosy. Somewhat ironically, a posthumous myth that London was a womanizing alcoholic who took his own life (despite his actual death of renal failure in 1916) would diminish the weight granted his body of work in the annals of literary and social history.

This Enriched Classics edition of Jack London's *The Call of the Wild* was prepared under the supervision of an editorial committee directed by Harry Shefter, professor of English at New York University. The illustrations are derived from original watercolors based upon authentic source materials depicting scenes contemporary with the time of the story.

TITLES AVAILABLE IN THE ENRICHED CLASSICS SERIES

Aristotle	*The Pocket Aristotle*, Edited by Justin D. Kaplan
Emily Brontë	*Wuthering Heights*
Pearl S. Buck	*The Good Earth*
Willa Cather	*My Ántonia*
Geoffrey Chaucer	*The Canterbury Tales*
Kate Chopin	*The Awakening*
Stephen Crane	*The Red Badge of Courage*
Charles Dickens	*Great Expectations*
	A Tale of Two Cities
F. Scott Fitzgerald	*This Side of Paradise*
Thomas Hardy	*Tess of the d'Urbervilles*
Nathaniel Hawthorne	*The Scarlet Letter*
Thor Heyerdahl	*Kon-Tiki*
Homer	*The Odyssey*
Henry James	*Washington Square*
James Joyce	*Dubliners*
	A Portrait of the Artist as a Young Man
John (Fire) Lame Deer and Richard Erdoes	*Lame Deer, Seeker of Visions*
Jack London	*The Call of the Wild*
Herman Melville	*Billy Budd, Sailor*
	Moby-Dick
Plato	*Dialogues of Plato*, Edited by Justin D. Kaplan
George Bernard Shaw	*Pygmalion*
Mary Shelley	*Frankenstein*
Sophocles	*Oedipus the King*
Robert Louis Stevenson	*Dr. Jekyll and Mr. Hyde*
Mark Twain	*Adventures of Huckleberry Finn*
	The Adventures of Tom Sawyer
Edith Wharton	*The Age of Innocence*
	Old New York

OTHER CLASSICS

F. Scott Fitzgerald	*The Beautiful and Damned*
	Flappers and Philosophers
Robert Frost	*Robert Frost's Poems*
Victor Hugo	*Les Misérables*
Franz Kafka	*The Basic Kafka*, Edited by Erich Heller
Karl Marx and Friedrich Engels	*The Communist Manifesto*
Edgar Allan Poe	*Great Tales and Poems of Edgar Allan Poe*
Jean-Paul Sartre	*Being and Nothingness*

The Call
of the Wild
and
Bâtard

JACK LONDON

Introduction by Earle Labor
and Jeanne Campbell Reesman

POCKET BOOKS

New York   London   Toronto   Sydney   Singapore

POCKET BOOKS, a division of Simon & Schuster, Inc.
1230 Avenue of the Americas, New York, NY 10020

Copyright 1903, 1926, 1931 by The MacMillan Company;
Reader's Supplement copyright © 1963, 1974 by
Simon & Schuster, Inc.

Supplementary material © 2001 by Simon & Schuster, Inc.

Introduction from *Jack London* by Earle Labor and Jeanne Campbell
Reesman, Twayne Publishers, 1994. Reprinted by permission of
The Gate Group.

All rights reserved, including the right to reproduce
this book or portions thereof in any form whatsoever.
For information address Pocket Books, 1230 Avenue
of the Americas, New York, NY 10020

ISBN: 0-671-70494-X

First Pocket Books printing November 1974

32 31 30 29 28 27

POCKET and colophon are registered trademarks of
Simon & Schuster, Inc.

For information regarding special discounts for bulk purchases,
please contact Simon & Schuster Special Sales at 1-800-456-6798 or
business@simonandschuster.com

Printed in the U.S.A.

CONTENTS

INTRODUCTION

❧

*From "Jack London: The Literary Frontiersman"**
by Earle Labor and Jeanne Campbell Reesman

Full appreciation of *The Call of the Wild* and *White Fang* begins with "Bâtard," London's first dog story, published in the June 1902 issue of *Cosmopolitan* under the euphemistic title "Diable—A Dog." Although its thematic relationship to the two later works is inverse, this fine tale shares with both of them the characteristics of fable and, especially with *White Fang*, the theme of hereditary and environmental determinism. "Bâtard" is an anatomy of hatred, and its canine protagonist— "Hell's Spawn," as he is called by some—is the antithesis of everything that man's best friend is supposed to be. It is clear that such devils are not merely born; they are also made:

Bâtard did not know his father—hence his name—but, as John Hamlin [the storekeeper of the Sixty Mile Post] knew, his father was a great

*Reprinted from Earle Labor and Jeanne Campbell Reesman. *Jack London.* New York: Twayne Publishers. Revised edition, 1994.

gray timber wolf. But the mother of Bâtard, as he
dimly remembered her, was a snarling, bickering,
obscene husky, full-fronted and heavy-chested,
with a malign eye, a cat-like grip on life, and a
genius for trickery and evil. . . . Much of evil and
much of strength were there in these, Bâtard's
progenitors, and, bone and flesh of their bone and
flesh, he had inherited it all. And then came Black
Leclère, to lay his heavy hand on the bit of pulsating puppy life, to press and prod and mould till it
became a big bristling beast, acute in knavery,
overspilling with hate, sinister, malignant, diabolical. With a proper master Bâtard might have made
an ordinary, fairly efficient sled-dog. He never got
the chance: Leclère but confirmed him in his congenital iniquity.

His sadistic treatment at the hand of his human antagonist, the dissolute voyageur, finally transforms Bâtard
into the incarnation of evil. Half-starved, tortured,
beaten, and cursed, the dog grows progressively more
vicious and cunning—yet he refuses to leave his master
because he bides with uncanny patience his time for re-
venge. Nor can Black Leclère resist his compulsion to
cultivate this hatred. Even after Bâtard has attacked
him in his sleep and has slit his throat, he refuses to ac-
cept the advice of old-timers who urge him to let them
shoot the dog. But Leclère is no match for the preternatural malevolence he has unleashed. Near the end of
the story, unjustly convicted of murdering a gold miner,
he is forced to mount a large box, hands tied and noose

around his neck. He gets a last-minute reprieve, but the miners leave him alone, standing precariously on the box, to meditate upon his sinful ways while they go downriver to apprehend the real murderer. When the miners have gone, the dog, grinning "with a fiendish levity in his bearing that Leclère [cannot] mistake," casually retreats a few yards—then hurls himself against the box on which his helpless master is standing. "Fifteen minutes later, Slackwater Charley and Webster Shaw, returning, caught a glimpse of a ghostly pendulum swinging back and forth in the dim light. As they hurriedly drew in closer, they made out the man's inert body, and a live thing that clung to it, and shook and worried, and gave to it the swaying motion."

London said he wrote *The Call of the Wild* to redeem the species. "I started it as a companion to my other dog story 'Bâtard,' which you may remember; but it got away from me, and instead of 4,000 words it ran 32,000 before I could call a halt." Joan London tells us that as far as her father was concerned, this masterpiece was "a purely fortuitous piece of work, a lucky shot in the dark that had unexpectedly found its mark," and that, when reviewers enthusiastically interpreted *The Call of the Wild* as a brilliant human allegory, he was astonished: " 'I plead guilty,' he admitted, 'but I was unconscious of it at the time. I did not mean to do it.' " However, he was not entirely oblivious to the story's unusual merit.

London's story was utterly different from the humanized beasts in Kipling's "Mowgli" stories and from the sentimental projections of Margaret Marshall Saunders's *Beautiful Joe* and Ernest Seton's *Biography of a*

Grizzly, which were enormously popular in London's day and are still found in the children's sections of libraries. Charles G. D. Roberts, writing about the appeal of such literature at the turn of the century, explained that "the animal story, as we now have it, is a potent emancipator. It frees us for a little while from the world of shop-worn utilities, and from the mean tenement of self of which we do well to grow weary. . . . It has ever the more significance, it has ever the richer gift of refreshment and renewal, the more humane the heart and spiritual the understanding which we bring to the intimacy of it."[1] This explanation holds true for *The Call of the Wild* as well as for the other wild animal stories: London's work offers the "gift of refreshment and renewal," as well as a certain escapism. The difference is its radical departure from the conventional animal story in style and substance—the manner in which it is, to use the psychoanalytic term, *overdetermined* in its multilayered meaning.[2]

Maxwell Geismar gives a clue to the deeper layer of meaning when he classifies the work as "a beautiful prose poem, or *nouvelle,* of gold and death on the instinctual level" and as a "handsome parable of the buried impulses."[3] We need only interpolate that these "buried impulses" are essentially human, not canine, and that readers identify more closely than they may realize with this protagonist. The plot is animated by one of the most basic of archetypal motifs: the Myth of the Hero. The call to adventure, departure, initiation, the perilous journey to the mysterious life-center, transformation, and apotheosis: these are the phases of the Myth; and all are present in Buck's progress from the civilized world through the natural and beyond to the supernatural world.[4] His journey carries him not only through space but also through time and, ultimately, into the still center of a world that is timeless.

Richard Chase points out that in the type of long fiction most properly designated as the *romance*, character becomes "somewhat abstract and ideal," and plot is "highly colored": "Astonishing events may occur, and these are likely to have a symbolic or ideological, rather than a realistic, plausibility. Being less committed to the immediate rendition of reality than the novel, the romance will more freely veer toward mythic, allegorical, and symbolistic forms."[5] All of these remarks are directly applicable to *The Call of the Wild*, in which the richly symbolistic form ultimately becomes the content of the fiction. The seven chapters of the work fall into four major parts or movements. Each of these movements is distinguished by its own theme, rhythm, and tone; each is climaxed by an event of dramatic intensity; and each marks a stage in the hero's transformation from a phenomenal into an ideal figure.

Part 1, consisting of three chapters, is, with its emphasis on physical violence and amoral survival, the most Naturalistic—and the most literal—of the book. Its rhythms are quick, fierce, muscular. Images of intense struggle, pain, and blood predominate. Chapter 1, "Into the Primitive," describes the great dog's kidnapping from Judge Miller's pastoral ranch and his subsequent endurance of the first rites of his initiation—the beginning of the transformation that ultimately carries him deep into Nature's heart of darkness: "For two days and nights he neither ate nor drank, and during those two days and nights of torment, he accumulated a fund of wrath that boded ill for whoever first fell foul of him. His eyes turned blood-shot, and he was metamorphosed into a raging fiend. So changed was he that the Judge himself would not have recognized him; and the express messengers breathed with relief when they bundled him off the train at Seattle."[6]

The high priest of Buck's first initiatory rites is the symbolic figure in the red sweater, the man with the club who relentlessly pounds the hero into a disciplined submission to the code of violence and toil. "Well, Buck, my boy," the man calmly observes after the merciless beating, "we've had our little ruction, and the best thing we can do is to let it go at that. You've learned your place, and I know mine." Like all of London's heroes who survive the rigors of the White Silence, Buck has passed the first test: that of adaptability.

Chapter 2, "The Law of Club and Fang," takes the hero to the Northland. On Dyea Beach he encounters the dogs and men who are to become his traveling companions in the long, hard months ahead. He also continues to absorb the lessons of survival. Curly, the most amiable of the newly arrived pack, is knocked down by a veteran husky, then ripped apart by the hordes of canine spectators. The scene remains vividly etched in Buck's memory: "So that was the way. No fair play. Once down, that was the end of you." Later, as he is broken into his traces for the trail, he awakens to the great driving motivation of the veteran sled dogs: the extraordinary love of toil. But more significant is the metamorphosis of his moral values. He learns, for example, that stealing, an unthinkable misdeed in his former state, can be the difference between survival and death: "It was all well enough in the Southland, under the law of love and fellowship, to respect private property and personal feelings; but in the Northland, under the law of club and fang, whoso took such things into account was a fool, and in so far as he observed them he would fail to prosper."

Chapter 3, "The Dominant Primordial Beast," marks the conclusion of the first major phase of Buck's initiation, for it reveals that he is not merely qualified as a member of the pack but that he is worthy of leadership. This chapter has a pronounced modulation of style to signal the glimmerings of Buck's mythic destiny; instead of sharply detailed physical description, we begin to encounter passages of tone poetry:

> With the aurora borealis flaming coldly overhead, or the stars leaping in the frost dance, and the land numb and frozen under its pall of snow, this song of the huskies might have been the defiance of life, only it was pitched in minor key, with long-drawn wailings and half-sobs, and was more the pleading of life, the articulate travail of existence. . . . When he moaned and sobbed, it was with the pain of living that was of old the pain of his wild fathers, and the fear and mystery of the cold and dark that was to them fear and mystery.

London's style becomes increasingly lyrical as the narrative rises from literal to symbolic level, and it reaches such intensity near the end of chapter 3 that we now realize Buck's is no common animal story:

There is an ecstasy that marks the summit of life, and beyond which life cannot rise. And such is the paradox of living, this ecstasy comes when one is most alive, and it comes as a complete forgetfulness that one is alive. This ecstasy, this forgetfulness of living, comes to the artist, caught up and out of himself in a sheet of flame; it comes to the soldier, war-mad on a stricken field and refusing quarter; and it came to Buck, leading the pack, sounding the old wolf-cry, straining after the food that was alive and that fled swiftly before him through the moonlight. He was sounding the deeps of his nature, and of the parts of his nature that were deeper than he, going back into the womb of Time. He was mastered by the sheer surging of life, the tidal wave of being, the perfect joy of each separate muscle, joint, and sinew in that it was everything that was not death, that it was aglow and rampant, expressing itself in movement, flying exultantly under the stars and over the face of dead matter that did not move.

This paragraph is a thematic epitome of the whole work, and it functions as a prologue to the weird moonlit scene in which Buck challenges Spitz for leadership of the team, a scene noted by Geismar as "a perfect instance of the 'son-horde' theory which Frazer traced in *The Golden Bough*, and of that primitive ritual to which Freud himself attributed both a sense of original sin and the fundamental ceremony of religious exorcism."

Even though Buck has now "Won to Mastership" (chapter 4), he is not ready for apotheosis. He is a leader and a hero—but he is not yet a god. His divinity must be confirmed, as prescribed by ritual, through death and re-birth. After the climactic pulsations of chapter 3, a slowing of beat occurs in the second movement. Death occurs symbolically, almost literally, in chapter 5 ("The Toil of Trace and Trail"). Clustering darkly, the dominant images are those of pain and fatigue as Buck and his teammates suffer under the ownership of the three *chechaquos*: Charles, his wife Mercedes, and her brother Hal—"a nice family party." Like the two Incapables of "In a Far Country," they display all the fatal symptoms of incompetence and unfitness: "Buck felt vaguely that there was no depending upon these two men and the woman. They did not know how to do anything, and as days went by it became apparent that they could not learn. They were slack in all things, without order or discipline." Without a sense of economy or the will to work and endure hardship themselves, they overwork, starve, and beat their dogs—then they turn on one another:

> Their irritability arose out of their misery, in-creased with it, doubled upon it, outdistanced it. The wonderful patience of the trail which comes to all men who toil hard and suffer sore, and re-main sweet of speech and kindly, did not come to

these two men and the woman. They had no
inkling of such a patience. They were stiff and in
pain; their muscles ached, their bones ached, their
very hearts ached; and because of this they became sharp of speech, and hard words were first
on their lips in the morning and last at night.

This ordeal is the second long and difficult phase of
Buck's initiation. The "long journey" is described in increasingly morbid imagery as the "perambulating skeletons" and "wayfarers of death" approach closer to their
fatal end in the thawing ice of Yukon River; the journey
ends with Buck's symbolic crucifixion as he is beaten
nearly to death by Hal shortly before the ghostly caravan moves on without him and disappears into the icy
maw of the river.

Buck's rebirth comes in chapter 6, "For the Love of a
Man," which also functions as the third and transitional
movement of the narrative. Having been rescued by John
Thornton, the benign helper who traditionally appears in
the Myth to lead the hero toward his goal, Buck is now
being readied for the final phase of his odyssey. Appropri-
ately, the season is spring; and the mood is idyllic as he
wins back his strength, "lying by the river bank through
the long spring days, watching the running water, listening
lazily to the songs of the birds and the hum of nature. . . ."
And, during this same convalescent period, the hints of his
destiny grow more insistent: "He was older than the days
he had seen and the breaths he had drawn. He linked the
past with the present, and the eternity behind him
throbbed through him in a mighty rhythm to which he

swayed as the tides and seasons swayed. . . . Deep in the forest a call was sounding. . . . But as often as he gained the soft unbroken earth and the green shade, the love for John Thornton drew him back. . . ." The passionate devotion of Thornton climaxes in the final scene of chapter 6 when Buck wins a $1,000 wager for his master by moving a half-ton sled 100 yards; this legendary feat, which concludes the third movement of the narrative, foreshadows the hero's supernatural appointment in the fourth and final movement.

Chapter 7, "The Sounding of the Call," consummates Buck's transformation. In keeping with this change, London shifts both the setting and the tone. Thornton, taking the money earned by Buck in the wager, begins his last quest "into the East after a fabled lost mine, the history of which was as old as the history of the country . . . steeped in tragedy and shrouded in mystery." As the small party moves into the wilderness, the scene assumes a mythic atmosphere and the caravan is enveloped in a strange aura of timelessness:

> The months came and went, and back and forth they twisted through the uncharted vastness, where no men were and yet where men had been if the Lost Cabin were true. They went across divides in summer blizzards, shivered under the midnight sun on naked mountains between the timber line and the eternal snows, dropped into summer valleys amid swarming gnats and flies, and in the shadows of glaciers picked strawberries and flowers as ripe and fair as any the Southland

could boast. In the fall of the year they penetrated a weird lake country, sad and silent, where wildfowl had been, but where then there was no life nor sign of life—only the blowing chill winds, the forming of ice in sheltered places, and the melancholy rippling of waves on lonely beaches.

The weirdness of the atmosphere is part of the "call to adventure" described by Joseph Campbell in *The Hero with a Thousand Faces,* which "signifies that destiny has summoned the hero and transferred his spiritual center of gravity from within the pale of society to a zone unknown. This fateful region of both treasure and danger may be variously represented: as a distant land, a forest, . . . or profound dream state; but it is always a place of strangely fluid and polymorphous beings, unimaginable torments, superhuman deeds and impossible delight." This "fateful region of both treasure and danger" is a far cry from Judge Miller's pastoral ranch and from the raw frontier of the Klondike gold rush: it is the landscape of myth. The party finally arrives at its destination, a mysterious and incredibly rich placer valley where "Like giants they toiled, days flashing on the heels of days like dreams as they heaped the treasure up."

His role fulfilled as guide into the unknown zone, Thornton and his party are killed by the savage Yeehats, and Buck is released from the bond of love to fulfill the last phase of his apotheosis as he is transformed into the immortal Ghost Dog of Northland legend. He incarnates the eternal mystery of creation and life: "[And when] the long winter nights come on and the wolves follow their meat into the lower valleys . . . a great, gloriously coated wolf, like, and yet unlike, all other wolves . . . may be seen running at the head of the pack through the pale moonlight or glimmering borealis, leaping gigantic above his fellows, his great throat abellow as he sings a song of the younger world, which is the song of the pack."

Although *The Call of the Wild* was perhaps no luckier than any other great artistic achievement, it was "a shot in the dark" in an unintended sense—into the dark wilderness of the unconscious. And as with other great literary works, its ultimate meaning eludes us. But at least a significant part of that meaning relates to the area of human experience that cannot be translated into discursive terms and that must therefore be approached tentatively and obliquely. After granting this much, we may infer that the animating force of London's wild romance is the vital energy Jung called *libido* and that London's hero is a projection of the reader's own *self* eternally striving for psychic integration in the process called *individuation*. Such an inference accounts for the appropriateness of London's division of his narrative into seven chapters that fall naturally into four movements, quarternity symbolizing, in Jung's words, "the ideal of completeness" and "the totality of the personality," and seven, the archetypal number of perfect order and the consummation of a cycle.[7] But, of course, we do not need such a technical explanation to know that the call to which we respond as the great Ghost Dog flashes through the glimmering borealis singing his song of the younger world is the faint but clear echo of a music deep within ourselves.

The artistic significance of *The Call of the Wild* was recognized at once in one of those rare instances when critical taste and popular appetite agree, and Jack London was acclaimed by the world as a major writer. During the years afterward, he had other moments of "primordial" inspiration, but none surpassed the sustained vision of this extraordinary "parable of the buried impulses."

---

1. Charles G. D. Roberts, *The Kindred of the Wild* (Boston: Page, 1902), 29.
2. See Simon O. Lesser, *Fiction and the Unconscious* (Boston: Beacon Press, 1957), 113.
3. Maxwell Geismar, ed., "Introduction," *Jack London: Short Stories*, American Century Series (New York: Hill & Wang, 1960), ix–x.
4. See Joseph Campbell, *The Hero with a Thousand Faces*, Meridian Ed. (New York: Meridian, 1956), 34–46.
5. Richard Chase, *The American Novel and Its Tradition*, Anchor Ed. (Garden City, N.Y.: Doubleday, 1957), 13.
6. *The Call of the Wild* (New York: Macmillan, 1903).
7. See J. E. Cirlot, *A Dictionary of Symbols*, trans. Jack Sage (New York: Philosophical Library, 1962), 223.

Bâtard

Bâtard was a devil. This was recognized throughout the Northland. "Hell's Spawn" he was called by many men, but his master, Black Leclère, chose for him the shameful name "Bâtard." Now Black Leclère was also a devil, and the twain were well matched. There is a saying that when two devils come together, hell is to pay. This is to be expected, and this certainly was to be expected when Bâtard and Black Leclère came together. The first time they met, Bâtard was a part-grown puppy, lean and hungry, with bitter eyes; and they met with snap and snarl, and wicked looks, for Leclère's upper lip had a wolfish way of lifting and showing the white, cruel teeth. And it lifted then, and his eyes glinted viciously, as he reached for Bâtard and dragged him out from the squirming litter. It was certain that they divined each other, for on the instant Bâtard had buried his puppy fangs in Leclère's hand, and Leclère, thumb and finger, was coolly choking his young life out of him.

"*Sacredam,*" the Frenchman said softly, flirting the

quick blood from his bitten hand and gazing down on the little puppy choking and gasping in the snow.

Leclère turned to John Hamlin, storekeeper of the Sixty Mile Post. "Dat fo' w'at Ah lak heem. 'Ow moch, eh, you, M'sieu'? 'Ow moch? Ah buy heem, now; Ah buy heem queek."

And because he hated him with an exceeding bitter hate, Leclère bought Bâtard and gave him his shameful name. And for five years the twain adventured across the Northland, from St. Michael's and the Yukon delta to the head-reaches of the Pelly and even so far as the Peace River, Athabasca, and the Great Slave. And they acquired a reputation for uncompromising wickedness, the like of which never before attached itself to man and dog.

Bâtard did not know his father—hence his name— but, as John Hamlin knew, his father was a great gray timber wolf. But the mother of Bâtard, as he dimly remembered her, was a snarling, bickering, obscene husky, full-fronted and heavy-chested, with a malign eye, a cat-like grip on life, and a genius for trickery and evil. There was neither faith nor trust in her. Her treachery alone could be relied upon, and her wild-wood amours attested her general depravity. Much of evil and much of strength were there in these, Bâtard's progenitors, and, bone and flesh of their bone and flesh, he had inherited it all. And then came Black Leclère, to lay his heavy hand on the bit of pulsating puppy life, to press and prod and mould till it became a big bristling beast, acute in knavery, overspilling with hate, sinister, malignant, diabolical. With a proper master Bâtard might have made an ordinary, fairly efficient sled-dog. He never got the chance: Leclère but confirmed him in his congenital iniquity.

The history of Bâtard and Leclère is a history of war—of five cruel, relentless years, of which their first meeting is fit summary. To begin with, it was Leclère's fault, for he hated with understanding and intelligence, while the long-legged, ungainly puppy hated only blindly, instinctively, without reason or method. At first there were no refinements of cruelty (these were to come later), but simple beatings and crude brutalities. In one of these Bâtard had an ear injured. He never regained control of the riven muscles, and ever after the ear drooped limply down to keep keen the memory of his tormentor. And he never forgot.

His puppyhood was a period of foolish rebellion. He was always worsted, but he fought back because it was his nature to fight back. And he was unconquerable. Yelping shrilly from the pain of lash and club, he none the less contrived always to throw in the defiant snarl, the bitter vindictive menace of his soul which fetched without fail more blows and beatings. But his was his mother's tenacious grip on life. Nothing could kill him. He flourished under misfortune, grew fat with famine, and out of his terrible struggle for life developed a preternatural intelligence. His were the stealth and cunning of the husky, his mother, and the fierceness and valor of the wolf, his father.

Possibly it was because of his father that he never wailed. His puppy yelps passed with his lanky legs, so that he became grim and taciturn, quick to strike, slow to warn. He answered curse with snarl, and blow with snap, grinning the while his implacable hatred; but never again, under the extremest agony, did Leclère bring from him the cry of fear nor of pain. This unconquerableness but fanned Leclère's wrath and stirred him to greater deviltries.

Did Leclère give Bâtard half a fish and to his mates whole ones, Bâtard went forth to rob other dogs of their fish. Also he robbed caches and expressed himself in a thousand rogueries, till he became a terror to all dogs and masters of dogs. Did Leclère beat Bâtard and fondle Babette—Babette who was not half the worker he was—why, Bâtard threw her down in the snow and broke her hind leg in his heavy jaws, so that Leclère was forced to shoot her. Likewise, in bloody battles, Bâtard mastered all his team-mates, set them the law of trail and forage, and made them live to the law he set.

In five years he heard but one kind word, received but one soft stroke of a hand, and then he did not know what manner of things they were. He leaped like the untamed thing he was, and his jaws were together in a flash. It was the missionary at Sunrise, a newcomer in the country, who spoke the kind word and gave the soft stroke of the hand. And for six months after, he wrote no letters home to the States, and the surgeon at McQuestion travelled two hundred miles on the ice to save him from blood-poisoning.

Men and dogs looked askance at Bâtard when he drifted into their camps and posts. The men greeted him with feet threateningly lifted for the kick, the dogs with bristling manes and bared fangs. Once a man did kick Bâtard, and Bâtard, with quick wolf snap, closed his jaws like a steel trap on the man's calf and crunched down to the bone. Whereat the man was determined to have his life, only Black Leclère, with ominous eyes and naked hunting-knife, stepped in between. The killing of Bâtard—ah, *sacredam, that* was a pleasure Leclère reserved for himself. Some day it would happen, or else—bah! who was to know? Anyway, the problem would be solved.

For they had become problems to each other. The very breath each drew was a challenge and a menace to the other. Their hate bound them together as love could never bind. Leclère was bent on the coming of the day when Bâtard should wilt in spirit and cringe and whimper at his feet. And Bâtard—Leclère knew what was in Bâtard's mind, and more than once had read it in Bâtard's eyes. And so clearly had he read, that when Bâtard was at his back, he made it a point to glance often over his shoulder.

Men marvelled when Leclère refused large money for the dog. "Some day you'll kill him and be out his price," said John Hamlin once, when Bâtard lay panting in the snow where Leclère had kicked him, and no one knew whether his ribs were broken, and no one dared look to see.

"Dat," said Leclère, dryly, "dat is my biz'ness, M'sieu'."

And the men marvelled that Bâtard did not run away. They did not understand. But Leclère understood. He was a man who lived much in the open, beyond the sound of human tongue, and he had learned the voices

of wind and storm, the sigh of night, the whisper of
dawn, the clash of day. In a dim way he could hear the
green things growing, the running of the sap, the bursting of the bud. And he knew the subtle speech of the
things that moved, of the rabbit in the snare, the moody
raven beating the air with hollow wing, the baldface
shuffling under the moon, the wolf like a gray shadow
gliding betwixt the twilight and the dark. And to him
Bâtard spoke clear and direct. Full well he understood
why Bâtard did not run away, and he looked more often
over his shoulder.

When in anger, Bâtard was not nice to look upon, and
more than once had he leapt for Leclère's throat, to be
stretched quivering and senseless in the snow, by the butt
of the ever ready dogwhip. And so Bâtard learned to bide
his time. When he reached his full strength and prime of
youth, he thought the time had come. He was broad-
chested, powerfully muscled, of far more than ordinary
size, and his neck from head to shoulders was a mass of
bristling hair—to all appearances a full-blooded wolf.
Leclère was lying asleep in his furs when Bâtard deemed
the time to be ripe. He crept upon him stealthily, head
low to earth and lone ear laid back, with a feline softness
of tread. Bâtard breathed gently, very gently, and not till
he was close at hand did he raise his head. He paused for
a moment, and looked at the bronzed bull throat, naked
and knotty, and swelling to a deep steady pulse. The
slaver dripped down his fangs and slid off his tongue at
the sight, and in that moment he remembered his drooping ear, his uncounted blows and prodigious wrongs, and
without a sound sprang on the sleeping man.

Leclère awoke to the pang of the fangs in his throat, and, perfect animal that he was, he awoke clear-headed and with full comprehension. He closed on Bâtard's windpipe with both his hands, and rolled out of his furs to get his weight upper-most. But the thousands of Bâtard's ancestors had clung at the throats of unnumbered moose and caribou and dragged them down, and the wisdom of those ancestors was his. When Leclère's weight came on top of him, he drove his hind legs upward and in, and clawed down chest and abdomen, ripping and tearing through skin and muscle. And when he felt the man's body wince above him and lift, he worried and shook at the man's throat. His team-mates closed around in a snarling circle, and Bâtard, with failing breath and fading sense, knew that their jaws were hungry for him. But that did not matter—it was the man, the man above him, and he ripped and clawed, and shook and worried, to the last ounce of his strength. But Leclère choked him with both his hands, till Bâtard's chest heaved and writhed for the air denied, and his eyes glazed and set, and his jaws slowly loosened, and his tongue protruded black and swollen.

"Eh? *Bon*, you devil!" Leclère gurgled, mouth and throat clogged with his own blood, as he shoved the dizzy dog from him.

And then Leclère cursed the other dogs off as they fell upon Bâtard. They drew back into a wider circle, squatting alertly on their haunches and licking their chops, the hair on every neck bristling and erect.

Bâtard recovered quickly, and at sound of Leclère's

voice, tottered to his feet and swayed weakly back and
forth.

"A-h-ah! You beeg devil!" Leclère spluttered. "Ah fix
you; Ah fix you plentee, by *Gar!*"

Bâtard, the air biting into his exhausted lungs like
wine, flashed full into the man's face, his jaws missing
and coming together with a metallic clip. They rolled
over and over on the snow, Leclère striking madly with
his fists. Then they separated, face to face, and circled
back and forth before each other. Leclère could have
drawn his knife. His rifle was at his feet. But the beast
in him was up and raging. He would do the thing with
his hands—and his teeth. Bâtard sprang in, but
Leclère knocked him over with a blow of the fist, fell
upon him, and buried his teeth to the bone in the dog's
shoulder.

It was a primordial setting and a primordial scene,
such as might have been in the savage youth of the
world. An open space in a dark forest, a ring of grinning
wolf-dogs, and in the centre two beasts, locked in combat, snapping and snarling, raging madly about, panting,
sobbing, cursing, straining, wild with passion, in a fury
of murder, ripping and tearing and clawing in elemental
brutishness.

But Leclère caught Bâtard behind the ear, with a
blow from his fist, knocking him over, and, for the
instant, stunning him. Then Leclère leaped upon him
with his feet, and sprang up and down, striving to
grind him into the earth. Both Bâtard's hind legs
were broken ere Leclère ceased that he might catch
breath.

"A-a-ah! A-a-ah!" he screamed, incapable of speech, shaking his fist, through sheer impotence of throat and larynx.

But Bâtard was indomitable. He lay there in a helpless welter, his lip feebly lifting and writhing to the snarl he had not the strength to utter. Leclère kicked him, and the tired jaws closed on the ankle, but could not break the skin.

Then Leclère picked up the whip and proceeded almost to cut him to pieces, at each stroke of the lash crying: "Dis taim Ah break you! Eh? By *Gar!* Ah break you!"

In the end, exhausted, fainting from loss of blood, he crumpled up and fell by his victim, and when the wolf-dogs closed in to take their vengeance, with his last consciousness dragged his body on top Bâtard to shield him from their fangs.

This occurred not far from Sunrise, and the missionary, opening the door to Leclère a few hours later, was surprised to note the absence of Bâtard from the team. Nor did his surprise lessen when Leclère threw back the robes from the sled, gathered Bâtard into his arms, and staggered across the threshold. It happened that the surgeon of McQuestion, who was something of a gadabout, was up on a gossip, and between them they proceeded to repair Leclère.

"*Merci, non,*" said he. "Do you fix firs' de dog. To die? *Non.* Eet is not good. Becos' heem Ah mus' yet break. Dat fo' w'at he mus' not die."

The surgeon called it a marvel, the missionary a miracle, that Leclère pulled through at all; and so weakened was he, that in the spring the fever got him, and he went on his back again. Bâtard had been in even worse plight, but his grip on life prevailed, and the bones of his hind legs knit, and his organs righted themselves, during the several weeks he lay strapped to the floor. And by the time Leclère, finally convalescent, sallow and shaky, took the sun by the cabin door, Bâtard had reasserted his supremacy among his kind, and brought not only his own team-mates but the missionary's dogs into subjection.

He moved never a muscle, nor twitched a hair, when, for the first time, Leclère tottered out on the missionary's arm, and sank down slowly and with infinite caution on the three-legged stool.

"*Bon!*" he said. "*Bon!* De good sun!" And he stretched out his wasted hands and washed them in the warmth.

Then his gaze fell on the dog, and the old light blazed back in his eyes. He touched the missionary lightly on the arm. "*Mon père,* dat is one beeg devil, dat Bâtard. You will bring me one pistol, so dat Ah drink de sun in peace."

And thenceforth for many days he sat in the sun before the cabin door. He never dozed, and the pistol lay always across his knees. Bâtard had a way, the first thing each day, of looking for the weapon in its wonted place. At the sight of it he would lift his lip faintly in token that he understood, and Leclère would lift his own lip in an answering grin. One day the missionary took note of the trick.

"Bless me!" he said. "I really believe the brute comprehends."

Leclère laughed softly. "Look you, *mon père.* Dat w'at Ah now spik, to dat does he lissen."

As if in confirmation, Bâtard just perceptibly wriggled his lone ear up to catch the sound.

"Ah say 'keel.' "

Bâtard growled deep down in his throat, the hair bristled along his neck, and every muscle went tense and expectant.

"Ah lift de gun, so, like dat." And suiting action to word, he sighted the pistol at Bâtard.

Bâtard, with a single leap, sideways, landed around the corner of the cabin out of sight.

"Bless me!" he repeated at intervals.

Leclère grinned proudly.

"But why does he not run away?"

The Frenchman's shoulders went up in the racial shrug that means all things from total ignorance to infinite understanding.

"Then why do you not kill him?"

Again the shoulders went up.

"Mon père," he said after a pause, "de taim is not yet. He is one beeg devil. Some taim Ah break heem, so, an' so, all to leetle bits. Hey? Some taim. *Bon!"*

A day came when Leclère gathered his dogs together and floated down in a bateau to Forty Mile, and on to the Porcupine, where he took a commission from the P. C. Company, and went exploring for the better part of a year. After that he poled up the Koyokuk to deserted Arctic City, and later came drifting back, from camp to camp, along the Yukon. And during the long months Bâtard was well lessoned. He learned many tortures, and, notably, the torture of hunger, the torture of thirst, the torture of fire, and, worst of all, the torture of music.

Like the rest of his kind, he did not enjoy music. It gave him exquisite anguish, racking him nerve by nerve, and ripping apart every fibre of his being. It made him howl, long and wolf-like, as when the wolves bay the stars on frosty nights. He could not help howling. It was his one weakness in the contest with Leclère, and it was his shame. Leclère, on the other hand, passionately loved music—as passionately as he loved strong drink. And when his soul clamored for expression, it usually uttered itself in one or the other of the two ways, and more usually in both ways. And when he had drunk, his brain a-lilt with unsung song and the devil in him aroused and rampant, his soul found its supreme utterance in torturing Bâtard.

"Now we will haf a leetle museek," he would say. "Eh? W'at you t'ink, Bâtard?"

It was only an old and battered harmonica, tenderly treasured and patiently repaired; but it was the best that money could buy, and out of its silver reeds he drew weird vagrant airs that men had never heard before. Then Bâtard, dumb of throat, with teeth tight clenched, would back away, inch by inch, to the farthest cabin corner. And Leclère, playing, playing, a stout club tucked under his arm, followed the animal up, inch by inch, step by step, till there was no further retreat.

At first Bâtard would crowd himself into the smallest possible space, grovelling close to the floor; but as the music came nearer and nearer, he was forced to uprear, his back jammed into the logs, his fore legs fanning the air as though to beat off the rippling waves of sound. He still kept his teeth together, but severe muscular contractions attacked his body, strange twitchings and jerkings, till he was all a-quiver and writhing in silent torment. As he lost control, his jaws spasmodically wrenched apart, and deep throaty vibrations issued forth, too low in the register of sound for human ear to catch. And then, nostrils distended, eyes dilated, hair bristling in helpless rage, arose the long wolf howl. It came with a slurring rush upward, swelling to a great heart-breaking burst of sound, and dying away in sadly cadenced woe—then the next rush upward, octave upon octave; the bursting heart; and the infinite sorrow and misery, fainting, fading, falling, and dying slowly away.

It was fit for hell. And Leclère, with fiendish ken, seemed to divine each particular nerve and heart-string, and with long wails and tremblings and sobbing minors to make it yield up its last shred of grief. It was frightful, and for twenty-four hours after, Bâtard was nervous and unstrung, starting at common sounds, tripping over his own shadow, but, withal, vicious and masterful with his team-mates. Nor did he show signs of a breaking spirit. Rather did he grow more grim and taciturn, biding his time with an inscrutable patience that began to puzzle and weigh upon Leclère. The dog would lie in the firelight, motionless, for hours, gazing straight before him at Leclère, and hating him with his bitter eyes.

Often the man felt that he had bucked against the

very essence of life—the unconquerable essence that swept the hawk down out of the sky like a feathered thunderbolt, that drove the great gray goose across the zones, that hurled the spawning salmon through two thousand miles of boiling Yukon flood. At such times he felt impelled to express his own unconquerable essence; and with strong drink, wild music, and Bâtard, he indulged in vast orgies, wherein he pitted his puny strength in the face of things, and challenged all that was, and had been, and was yet to be.

"Dere is somet'ing dere," he affirmed, when the rhythmed vagaries of his mind touched the secret chords of Bâtard's being and brought forth the long lugubrious howl. "Ah pool eet out wid bot' my han's, so, an' so. Ha! Ha! Eet is fonee! Eet is ver' fonee! De priest chant, de womans pray, de mans swear, de leetle bird go *peep-peep*, Bâtard, heem go *yow-yow*—an' eet is all de ver' same t'ing. Ha! Ha!"

Father Gautier, a worthy priest, once reproved him with instances of concrete perdition. He never reproved him again.

"Eet may be so, *mon père*," he made answer. "An' Ah t'ink Ah go troo hell a-snappin', lak de hemlock troo de fire. Eh, *mon père?*"

But all bad things come to an end as well as good, and so with Black Leclère. On the summer low water, in a poling boat, he left McDougall for Sunrise. He left McDougall in company with Timothy Brown, and arrived at Sunrise by himself. Further, it was known that they had quarrelled just previous to pulling out; for the *Lizzie*, a wheezy ten-ton sternwheeler, twenty-four

hours behind, beat Leclère in by three days. And when
he did get in, it was with a clean-drilled bullet-hole
through his shoulder muscle, and a tale of ambush and
murder.

A strike had been made at Sunrise, and things had
changed considerably. With the infusion of several
hundred gold-seekers, a deal of whiskey, and half a
dozen equipped gamblers, the missionary had seen the
page of his years of labor with the Indians wiped clean.
When the squaws became preoccupied with cooking
beans and keeping the fire going for the wifeless miners, and the bucks with swapping their warm furs for
black bottles and broken timepieces, he took to his
bed, said "bless me" several times, and departed to his
final accounting in a rough-hewn, oblong box. Whereupon the gamblers moved their roulette and faro tables into the mission house, and the click of chips and
clink of glasses went up from dawn till dark and to
dawn again.

Now Timothy Brown was well beloved among these
adventurers of the north. The one thing against him was
his quick temper and ready fist—a little thing, for which
his kind heart and forgiving hand more than atoned. On
the other hand, there was nothing to atone for Black
Leclère. He was "black," as more than one remembered
deed bore witness, while he was as well hated as the
other was beloved. So the men of Sunrise put an anti-
septic dressing on his shoulder and haled him before
Judge Lynch.

It was a simple affair. He had quarrelled with Timothy Brown at McDougall. With Timothy Brown he had

left McDougall. Without Timothy Brown he had arrived at Sunrise. Considered in the light of his evilness, the unanimous conclusion was that he had killed Timothy Brown. On the other hand, Leclère acknowledged their facts, but challenged their conclusion, and gave his own explanation. Twenty miles out of Sunrise he and Timothy Brown were poling the boat along the rocky shore. From that shore two rifle-shots rang out. Timothy Brown pitched out of the boat and went down bubbling red, and that was the last of Timothy Brown. He, Leclère, pitched into the bottom of the boat with a stinging shoulder. He lay very quiet, peeping at the shore. After a time two Indians stuck up their heads and came out to the water's edge, carrying between them a birch-bark canoe. As they launched it, Leclère let fly. He potted one, who went over the side after the manner of Timothy Brown. The other dropped into the bottom of the canoe, and then canoe and poling boat went down the stream in a drifting battle. After that they hung up on a split current, and the canoe passed on one side of an island, the poling boat on the other. That was the last of the canoe, and he came on into Sunrise. Yes, from the way the Indian canoe jumped, he was sure he had potted him. That was all.

This explanation was not deemed adequate. They gave him ten hours' grace while the *Lizzie* steamed down to investigate. Ten hours later she came wheezing back to Sunrise. There had been nothing to investigate. No evidence had been found to back up his statements. They told him to make his will, for he possessed a fifty-thousand-dollar Sunrise claim, and they were a law-abiding as well as a law-giving breed.

Leclère shrugged his shoulders. "Bot one t'ing," he said; "a leetle, w'at you call, favor—a leetle favor, dat is eet. I gif my feefty t'ousan' dollair to de church. I gif my husky dog, Bâtard, to de devil. De leetle favor? Firs' you hang heem, an' den you hang me. Eet is good, eh?"

Good it was, they agreed, that Hell's Spawn should break trail for his master across the last divide, and the court was adjourned down to the river bank, where a big spruce tree stood by itself. Slackwater Charley put a hangman's knot in the end of a hauling-line, and the noose was slipped over Leclère's head and pulled tight around his neck. His hands were tied behind his back, and he was assisted to the top of a cracker box. Then the running end of the line was passed over an overhanging branch, drawn taut, and made fast. To kick the box out from under would leave him dancing on the air.

"Now for the dog," said Webster Shaw, sometime mining engineer. "You'll have to rope him, Slackwater."

Leclère grinned. Slackwater took a chew of tobacco, rove a running noose, and proceeded leisurely to coil a few turns in his hand. He paused once or twice to brush particularly offensive mosquitoes from off his face. Everybody was brushing mosquitoes, except Leclère, about whose head a small cloud was visible. Even Bâtard, lying full-stretched on the ground, with his forepaws rubbed the pests away from eyes and mouth.

But while Slackwater waited for Bâtard to lift his

head, a faint call came down the quiet air, and a man was seen waving his arms and running across the flat from Sunrise. It was the storekeeper.

"C-call 'er off, boys," he panted, as he came in among them.

"Little Sandy and Bernadotte's jes' got in," he explained with returning breath. "Landed down below an' come up by the short cut. Got the Beaver with 'm. Picked 'm up in his canoe, stuck in a back channel, with a couple of bullet holes in 'm. Other buck was Klok-Kutz, the one that knocked spots out of his squaw and dusted."

"Eh? W'at Ah say? Eh?" Leclère cried exultantly. "Dat de one fo' sure! Ah know. Ah spik true."

"The thing to do is teach these damned Siwashes a little manners," spoke Webster Shaw. "They're getting fat and sassy, and we'll have to bring them down a peg. Round in all the bucks and string up the Beaver for an object lesson. That's the programme. Come on and let's see what he's got to say for himself."

"Heh, M'sieu'!" Leclère called, as the crowd began to melt away through the twilight in the direction of Sunrise. "Ah lak ver' moch to see de fon."

"Oh, we'll turn you loose when we come back," Webster Shaw shouted over his shoulder. "In the meantime meditate on your sins and the ways of providence. It will do you good, so be grateful."

As is the way with men who are accustomed to great hazards, whose nerves are healthy and trained to patience, so it was with Leclère, who settled himself to the long wait—which is to say that he reconciled his mind to it. There was no settling of the body, for the taut rope forced him to stand rigidly erect. The least relaxation of the leg muscles pressed the rough-fibred noose into his neck, while the upright position caused him much pain in his wounded shoulder. He projected his under lip and expelled his breath upward along his face, to blow the mosquitoes away from his eyes. But the situation had its compensation. To be snatched from the maw of death was well worth a little bodily suffering, only it was unfortunate that he should miss the hanging of the Beaver.

And so he mused, till his eyes chanced to fall upon Bâtard, head between forepaws and stretched on the ground asleep. And then Leclère ceased to muse. He studied the animal closely, striving to sense if the sleep were real or feigned. Bâtard's sides were heaving regularly, but Leclère felt that the breath came and went a shade too quickly; also he felt that there was a vigilance or alertness to every hair that belied unshackling sleep. He would have given his Sunrise claim to be assured that the dog was not awake, and once, when one of his joints cracked, he looked quickly and guiltily at Bâtard to see if he roused. He did not rouse then, but a few minutes later he got up slowly and lazily, stretched, and looked carefully about him.

"Sacredam," said Leclère, under his breath. Assured that no one was in sight or hearing, Bâtard sat down, curled his upper lip almost into a smile, looked up at Leclère, and licked his chops.

"Ah see my feenish," the man said, and laughed sardonically aloud.

Bâtard came nearer, the useless ear wabbling, the good ear cocked forward with devilish comprehension. He thrust his head on one side quizzically, and advanced with mincing, playful steps. He rubbed his body gently against the box till it shook and shook again. Leclère teetered carefully to maintain his equilibrium.

"Bâtard," he said calmly, "look out. Ah keel you."

Bâtard snarled at the word, and shook the box with greater force. Then he upreared, and with his forepaws threw his weight against it higher up. Leclère kicked out with one foot, but the rope bit into his neck and checked so abruptly as nearly to overbalance him.

"Hi, ya! *Chook! Mush-on!*" he screamed.

Bâtard retreated, for twenty feet or so, with a fiendish levity in his bearing that Leclère could not mistake. He remembered the dog often breaking the scum of ice on the water hole, by lifting up and throwing his weight upon it; and, remembering, he understood what he now had in mind. Bâtard faced about and paused. He showed his white teeth in a grin, which Leclère answered; and then hurled his body through the air, in full charge, straight for the box.

Fifteen minutes later, Slackwater Charley and Webster Shaw, returning, caught a glimpse of a ghostly pendulum swinging back and forth in the dim light. As they hurriedly drew in closer, they made out the man's inert body, and a live thing that clung to it, and shook and worried, and gave to it the swaying motion.

"Hi, ya! *Chook!* you Spawn of Hell," yelled Webster Shaw.

But Bâtard glared at him, and snarled threateningly, without loosing his jaws.

Slackwater Charley got out his revolver, but his hand was shaking, as with a chill, and he fumbled.

"Here, you take it," he said, passing the weapon over.

Webster Shaw laughed shortly, drew a sight between the gleaming eyes, and pressed the trigger. Bâtard's body twitched with the shock, threshed the ground spasmodically for a moment, and went suddenly limp. But his teeth still held fast locked.

The Call of the Wild

❧

1

INTO THE PRIMITIVE

"Old longings nomadic leap,
Chafing at custom's chain;
Again from its brumal sleep
Wakens the ferine strain."

Buck did not read the newspapers, or he would have
known that trouble was brewing, not alone for himself,
but for every tidewater dog, strong of muscle and with
warm, long hair, from Puget Sound to San Diego. Because men, groping in the Arctic darkness, had found a
yellow metal, and because steamship and transportation
companies were booming the find, thousands of men
were rushing into the Northland. These men wanted
dogs, and the dogs they wanted were heavy dogs, with
strong muscles by which to toil, and furry coats to pro-
tect them from the frost.

Buck lived at a big house in the sun-kissed Santa
Clara Valley. Judge Miller's place, it was called. It stood
back from the road, half hidden among the trees,
through which glimpses could be caught of the wide
cool veranda that ran around its four sides. The house
was approached by gravelled driveways which wound
about through wide-spreading lawns and under the in-

terlacing boughs of tall poplars. At the rear things were on even a more spacious scale than at the front. There were great stables, where a dozen grooms and boys held forth, rows of vine-clad servants' cottages, an endless and orderly array of outhouses, long grape arbors, green pastures, orchards, and berry patches. Then there was the pumping plant for the artesian well, and the big cement tank where Judge Miller's boys took their morning plunge and kept cool in the hot afternoon.

And over this great demesne Buck ruled. Here he was born, and here he had lived the four years of his life. It was true, there were other dogs. There could not but be other dogs on so vast a place, but they did not count. They came and went, resided in the populous kennels, or lived obscurely in the recesses of the house after the fashion of Toots, the Japanese pug, or Ysabel, the Mexican hairless—strange creatures that rarely put nose out of doors or set foot to ground. On the other hand, there were the fox terriers, a score of them at least, who yelped fearful promises at Toots and Ysabel looking out of the windows at them and protected by a legion of housemaids armed with brooms and mops.

But Buck was neither house-dog nor kennel dog. The whole realm was his. He plunged into the swimming tank or went hunting with the Judge's sons; he escorted Mollie and Alice, the Judge's daughters, on long twilight or early morning rambles; on wintry nights he lay at the Judge's feet before the roaring library fire; he carried the Judge's grandsons on his back, or rolled them in the grass, and guarded their footsteps through wild adventures down to the fountain in the stable yard, and even beyond, where the paddocks were, and the berry patches. Among the terriers he stalked imperiously, and Toots and Ysabel he utterly ignored, for he was king— king over all creeping, crawling, flying things of Judge Miller's place, humans included.

His father, Elmo, a huge St. Bernard, had been the Judge's inseparable companion, and Buck bid fair to follow in the way of his father. He was not so large—he weighed only one hundred and forty pounds—for his mother, Shep, had been a Scotch shepherd dog. Nevertheless, one hundred and forty pounds, to which was added the dignity that comes of good living and universal respect, enabled him to carry himself in right royal fashion. During the four years since his puppyhood he had lived the life of a sated aristocrat; he had a fine pride in himself, was ever a trifle egotistical, as country gentlemen sometimes become because of their insular situation. But he had saved himself by not becoming a mere pampered house-dog. Hunting and kindred outdoor delights had kept down the fat and hardened his muscles; and to him, as to the cold-tubbing races, the love of water had been a tonic and a health preserver.

And this was the manner of dog Buck was in the fall of 1897, when the Klondike strike dragged men from all the world into the frozen North. But Buck did not read the newspapers, and he did not know that Manuel, one of the gardener's helpers, was an undesirable acquaintance. Manuel had one besetting sin. He loved to play Chinese lottery.[1] Also, in his gambling, he had one besetting weakness—faith in a system; and this made his damnation certain. For to play a system requires money, while the wages of a gardener's helper do not lap over the needs of a wife and numerous progeny.

The Judge was at a meeting of the Raisin Growers' Association, and the boys were busy organizing an athletic club, on the memorable night of Manuel's treachery. No one saw him and Buck go off through the orchard on what Buck imagined was merely a stroll. And with the exception of a solitary man, no one saw them arrive at the little flag station known as College Park. This man talked with Manuel, and money chinked between them.

"You might wrap up the goods before you deliver 'm," the stranger said gruffly, and Manuel doubled a piece of stout rope around Buck's neck under the collar.

"Twist it, an' you'll choke 'm plentee," said Manuel, and the stranger grunted a ready affirmative.

Buck had accepted the rope with quiet dignity. To be sure, it was an unwonted performance: but he had learned to trust in men he knew, and to give them credit for a wisdom that outreached his own. But when the ends of the rope were placed in the stranger's hands, he growled menacingly. He had merely intimated his displeasure, in his pride believing that to intimate was to command. But to his surprise the rope tightened around his neck, shutting off his breath. In quick rage he sprang at the man, who met him halfway, grappled him close by the throat, and with a deft twist threw him over on his back. Then the rope tightened mercilessly, while Buck struggled in a fury, his tongue lolling out of his mouth and his great chest panting futilely. Never in all his life had he been so vilely treated, and never in all his life had he been so angry. But his strength ebbed, his eyes glazed, and he knew nothing when the train was flagged and the two men threw him into the baggage car.

The next he knew, he was dimly aware that his tongue was hurting and that he was being jolted along in some kind of a conveyance. The hoarse shriek of a locomotive whistling a crossing told him where he was. He had travelled too often with the Judge not to know the sensation of riding in a baggage car. He opened his eyes, and into them came the unbridled anger of a kidnapped king. The man sprang for his throat, but Buck was too quick for him. His jaws closed on the hand, nor did they relax till his senses were choked out of him once more.

"Yep, has fits," the man said, hiding his mangled hand from the baggageman, who had been attracted by the sounds of struggle. "I'm takin' 'm up for the boss to 'Frisco. A crack dog-doctor there thinks that he can cure 'm."

Concerning that night's ride, the man spoke most eloquently for himself, in a little shed back of a saloon on the San Francisco water front.

"All I get is fifty for it," he grumbled; "an' I wouldn't do it over for a thousand, cold cash."

His hand was wrapped in a bloody handkerchief, and the right trouser leg was ripped from knee to ankle.

"How much did the other mug get?" the saloon-keeper demanded.

"A hundred," was the reply. "Wouldn't take a sou less, so help me."

"That makes a hundred and fifty," the saloon-keeper calculated; "and he's worth it, or I'm a squarehead."

The kidnapper undid the bloody wrappings and looked at his lacerated hand. "If I don't get the hydrophoby—"[2]

"It'll be because you was born to hang," laughed the saloon-keeper. "Here lend me a hand before you pull your freight," he added.

Dazed, suffering intolerable pain from throat and tongue, with the life half throttled out of him, Buck attempted to face his tormentors. But he was thrown down and choked repeatedly, till they succeeded in filing the heavy brass collar from off his neck. Then the rope was removed, and he was flung into a cagelike crate.

There he lay for the remainder of the weary night, nursing his wrath and wounded pride. He could not understand what it all meant. What did they want with him, these strange men? Why were they keeping him pent up in this narrow crate? He did not know why, but he felt oppressed by the vague sense of impending calamity. Several times during the night he sprang to his feet when the shed door rattled open, expecting to see the Judge, or the boys at least. But each time it was the bulging face of the saloon-keeper that peered in at him by the sickly light of a tallow candle. And each time the joyful bark that trembled in Buck's throat was twisted into a savage growl.

But the saloon-keeper let him alone, and in the morning four men entered and picked up the crate. More tormentors, Buck decided, for they were evil-looking creatures, ragged and unkempt; and he stormed and raged at them through the bars. They only laughed and poked sticks at him, which he promptly assailed with his teeth till he realized that that was what they wanted. Whereupon he lay down sullenly and allowed the crate to be lifted into a wagon. Then he, and the crate in which he was imprisoned, began a passage through many hands. Clerks in the express office took charge of him; he was carted about in another wagon; a truck carried him, with an assortment of boxes and parcels, upon a ferry steamer; he was trucked off the steamer into a great railway depot, and finally he was deposited in an express car.

For two days and nights this express car was dragged along at the tail of shrieking locomotives; and for two days and nights Buck neither ate nor drank. In his anger he had met the first advances of the express messengers with growls, and they had retaliated by teasing him. When he flung himself against the bars, quivering and frothing, they laughed at him and taunted him. They growled and barked like detestable dogs, mewed, and flapped their arms and crowed. It was all very silly, he knew; but therefore the more outrage to his dignity, and his anger waxed and waxed. He did not mind the hunger so much, but the lack of water caused him severe suffering and fanned his wrath to fever-pitch. For that matter, high-strung and finely sensitive, the ill treatment had flung him into a fever, which was fed by the inflammation of his parched and swollen throat and tongue.

He was glad for one thing: the rope was off his neck. That had given them an unfair advantage; but now that it was off, he would show them. They would never get another rope around his neck. Upon that he was resolved. For two days and nights he neither ate nor drank, and during those two days and nights of torment, he accumulated a fund of wrath that boded ill for whoever first fell foul of him. His eyes turned blood-shot, and he was metamorphosed into a raging fiend. So changed was he that the Judge himself would not have recognized him; and the express messengers breathed with relief when they bundled him off the train at Seattle.

Four men gingerly carried the crate from the wagon into a small, high-walled back yard. A stout man, with a red sweater that sagged generously at the neck, came out and signed the book for the driver. That was the man, Buck divined, the next tormentor, and he hurled himself savagely against the bars. The man smiled grimly, and brought a hatchet and a club.

"You ain't going to take him out now?" the driver asked.

"Sure," the man replied, driving the hatchet into the crate for a pry.

There was an instantaneous scattering of the four men who had carried it in, and from safe perches on top the wall they prepared to watch the performance.

Buck rushed at the splintering wood, sinking his teeth into it, surging and wrestling with it. Wherever the hatchet fell on the outside, he was there on the inside, snarling and growling, as furiously anxious to get out as the man in the red sweater was calmly intent on getting him out.

"Now, you red-eyed devil," he said, when he had made an opening sufficient for the passage of Buck's body. At the same time he dropped the hatchet and shifted the club to his right hand.

And Buck was truly a red-eyed devil, as he drew him-self together for the spring, hair bristling, mouth foaming, a mad glitter in his blood-shot eyes. Straight at the man he launched his one hundred and forty pounds of fury, surcharged with the pent passion of two days and nights. In mid air, just as his jaws were about to close on the man, he received a shock that checked his body and brought his teeth together with an agonizing clip. He whirled over, fetching the ground on his back and side. He had never been struck by a club in his life, and did not understand. With a snarl that was part bark and more scream he was again on his feet and launched into the air. And again the shock came and he was brought crushingly to the ground. This time he was aware that it was the club, but his madness knew no caution. A dozen times he charged, and as often the club broke the charge and smashed him down.

After a particularly fierce blow he crawled to his feet, too dazed to rush. He staggered limply about, the blood flowing from nose and mouth and ears, his beautiful coat sprayed and flecked with bloody slaver. Then the man advanced and deliberately dealt him a frightful blow on the nose. All the pain he had endured was as nothing compared with the exquisite agony of this. With a roar that was almost lionlike in its ferocity, he again hurled himself at the man. But the man, shifting the club from right to left, coolly caught him by the under jaw, at the same time wrenching downward and backward. Buck described a complete circle in the air, and half of another, then crashed to the ground on his head and chest.

For the last time he rushed. The man struck the shrewd blow he had purposely withheld for so long, and

Buck crumpled up and went down, knocked utterly senseless.

"He's no slouch at dog-breakin', that's wot I say," one of the men on the wall cried enthusiastically.

"Druther break cayuses any day, and twice on Sundays," was the reply of the driver, as he climbed on the wagon and started the horses.

Buck's senses came back to him, but not his strength. He lay where he had fallen, and from there he watched the man in the red sweater.

" 'Answers to the name of Buck,' " the man soliloquized, quoting from the saloon-keeper's letter which had announced the consignment of the crate and contents. "Well, Buck, my boy," he went on in a genial voice, "we've had our little ruction, and the best thing we can do is to let it go at that. You've learned your place, and I know mine. Be a good dog and all 'll go well and the goose hang high.[3] Be a bad dog, and I'll whale the stuffin' outa you. Understand?"

As he spoke he fearlessly patted the head he had so mercilessly pounded, and though Buck's hair involuntarily bristled at touch of the hand, he endured it without protest. When the man brought him water he drank eagerly, and later bolted a generous meal of raw meat, chunk by chunk, from the man's hand.

He was beaten (he knew that); but he was not broken. He saw, once for all, that he stood no chance against a man with a club. He had learned the lesson, and in all his after life he never forgot it. That club was a revelation. It was his introduction to the reign of primitive law, and he met the introduction halfway. The facts of life took on a fiercer aspect; and while he faced that aspect uncowed, he faced it with all the latent cunning of his nature aroused. As the days went by, other dogs came, in crates and at the ends of ropes, some docilely, and some raging and roaring as he had come; and, one and all, he watched them pass under the dominion of the man in the red sweater. Again and again, as he looked at each brutal performance, the lesson was driven home to Buck[4]: a man with a club was a law-giver, a master to be obeyed, though not necessarily conciliated. Of this last Buck was never guilty, though he did see beaten dogs that fawned upon the man, and wagged their tails, and licked his hand. Also he saw one dog, that would neither conciliate nor obey, finally killed in the struggle for mastery.

Now and again men came, strangers, who talked excitedly, wheedling, and in all kinds of fashions to the man in the red sweater. And at such times that money passed between them the strangers took one or more of the dogs away with them. Buck wondered where they went, for they never came back; but the fear of the future was strong upon him, and he was glad each time when he was not selected.

Yet his time came, in the end, in the form of a little weazened man who spat broken English and many strange and uncouth exclamations which Buck could not understand.

"Sacredam!" he cried, when his eyes lit upon Buck. "Dat one dam bully dog![5] Eh? How moch?"

"Three hundred, and a present at that," was the prompt reply of the man in the red sweater. "And seein' it's government money, you ain't got no kick coming, eh, Perrault?"

Perrault grinned. Considering that the price of dogs had been boomed skyward by the unwonted demand, it was not an unfair sum for so fine an animal. The Canadian Government would be no loser, nor would its despatches travel the slower. Perrault knew dogs, and when he looked at Buck he knew that he was one in a thousand— "One in ten t'ousand," he commented mentally.

Buck saw money pass between them, and was not surprised when Curly, a good-natured Newfoundland, and he were led away by the little weazened man. That was the last he saw of the man in the red sweater, and as Curly and he looked at receding Seattle from the deck of the *Narwhal*, it was the last he saw of the warm Southland. Curly and he were taken below by Perrault and turned over to a black-faced giant called François. Perrault was a French-Canadian, and swarthy; but François was a French-Canadian half-breed, and twice as swarthy. They were a new kind of men to Buck (of which he was destined to see many more), and while he developed no affection for them, he none the less grew honestly to respect them. He speedily learned that Perrault and François were fair men, calm and impartial in administering justice, and too wise in the way of dogs to be fooled by dogs.

In the 'tween-decks of the *Narwhal*, Buck and Curly joined two other dogs. One of them was a big, snow-white fellow from Spitzbergen who had been brought away by a whaling captain, and who had later accompanied a Geological Survey into the Barrens.

He was friendly, in a treacherous sort of way, smiling into one's face the while he meditated some underhand trick, as, for instance, when he stole from Buck's food at the first meal. As Buck sprang to punish him, the lash of François's whip sang through the air, reaching the culprit first; and nothing remained to Buck but to recover the bone. That was fair of François, he decided, and the half-breed began his rise in Buck's estimation.

The other dog made no advances, nor received any; also, he did not attempt to steal from the newcomers. He was a gloomy, morose fellow, and he showed Curly plainly that all he desired was to be left alone, and further, that there would be trouble if he were not left alone. "Dave" he was called, and he ate and slept, or yawned between times, and took interest in nothing, not even when the *Narwhal* crossed Queen Charlotte Sound and rolled and pitched and bucked like a thing possessed. When Buck and Curly grew excited, half wild with fear, he raised his head as though annoyed, favored them with an incurious glance, yawned, and went to sleep again.

Day and night the ship throbbed to the tireless pulse of the propeller, and though one day was very like another, it was apparent to Buck that the weather was steadily growing colder. At last, one morning, the propeller was quiet, and the *Narwhal* was pervaded with an atmosphere of excitement. He felt it, as did the other dogs, and knew that a change was at hand. François leashed them and brought them on deck. At the first step upon the cold surface, Buck's feet sank into white mushy something very like mud. He sprang back with a snort. More of this white stuff was falling through the air. He shook himself, but more of it fell upon him. He sniffed it curiously, then licked some up on his tongue. It bit like fire, and the next instant was gone. This puzzled him. He tried it again, with the same result. The onlookers laughed uproariously, and he felt ashamed, he knew not why, for it was his first snow.

2

※

THE LAW OF CLUB AND FANG

Buck's first day on the Dyea beach was like a nightmare. Every hour was filled with shock and surprise. He had been suddenly jerked from the heart of civilization and flung into the heart of things primordial. No lazy, sun-kissed life was this, with nothing to do but loaf and be bored. Here was neither peace, nor rest, nor a moment's safety. All was confusion and action, and every moment life and limb were in peril. There was imperative need to be constantly alert; for these dogs and men were not town dogs and men. They were savages, all of them, who knew no law but the law of club and fang.

He had never seen dogs fight as these wolfish creatures fought, and his first experience taught him an unforgettable lesson. It is true, it was a vicarious experience, else he would not have lived to profit by it. Curly was the victim. They were camped near the log store, where she, in her friendly way, made advances to a husky dog the size of a full-grown wolf, though not half so large as she. There was no warning, only a leap in like

41

a flash, a metallic clip of teeth, a leap out equally swift, and Curly's face was ripped open from eye to jaw.

It was the wolf manner of fighting, to strike and leap away; but there was more to it than this. Thirty or forty huskies ran to the spot and surrounded the combatants in an intent and silent circle. Buck did not comprehend that silent intentness, nor the eager way with which they were licking their chops. Curly rushed her antagonist, who struck again and leaped aside. He met her next rush with his chest, in a peculiar fashion that tumbled her off her feet. She never regained them. This was what the onlooking huskies had waited for. They closed in upon her, snarling and yelping, and she was buried, screaming with agony, beneath the bristling mass of bodies.

So sudden was it, and so unexpected, that Buck was taken aback. He saw Spitz run out his scarlet tongue in a way he had of laughing; and he saw François, swinging an axe, spring into the mess of dogs. Three men with clubs were helping him to scatter them. It did not take long. Two minutes from the time Curly went down, the last of her assailants were clubbed off. But she lay there limp and lifeless in the bloody, trampled snow, almost literally torn to pieces, the swart half-breed standing over her and cursing horribly. The scene often came back to Buck to trouble him in his sleep. So that was the way. No fair play. Once down, that was the end of you. Well, he would see to it that he never went down. Spitz ran out his tongue and laughed again, and from that moment Buck hated him with a bitter and deathless hatred.

Before he had recovered from the shock caused by the tragic passing of Curly, he received another shock.

François fastened upon him an arrangement of straps and buckles. It was a harness, such as he had seen the grooms put on the horses at home. And as he had seen horses work, so he was set to work, hauling François on a sled to the forest that fringed the valley, and returning with a load of firewood. Though his dignity was sorely hurt by thus being made a draught animal, he was too wise to rebel. He buckled down with a will and did his best, though it was all new and strange. François was stern, demanding instant obedience, and by virtue of his whip receiving instant obedience; while Dave, who was an experienced wheeler, nipped Buck's hind quarters whenever he was in error. Spitz was the leader, likewise experienced, and while he could not always get at Buck, he growled sharp reproof now and again, or cunningly threw his weight in the traces to jerk Buck into the way he should go. Buck learned easily, and under the combined tuition of his two mates and François made remarkable progress. Ere they returned to camp he knew enough to stop at "ho," to go ahead at "mush," to swing wide on the bends, and to keep clear of the wheeler when the loaded sled shot downhill at their heels.

"T'ree vair' good dogs,"[6] François told Perrault. "Dat Buck, heem pool lak hell. I tich heem queek as anyt'ing."

By afternoon, Perrault, who was in a hurry to be on the trail with his despatches, returned with two more dogs. "Billee" and "Joe," he called them, two brothers, and true huskies both. Sons of the one mother though they were, they were as different as day and night. Billee's one fault was his excessive good nature, while Joe was the very opposite, sour and introspective, with a perpetual snarl and a malignant eye. Buck received them in comradely fashion, Dave ignored them, while Spitz proceeded to thrash first one and then the other. Billee wagged his tail appeasingly, turned to run when he saw that appeasement was of no avail, and cried (still appeasingly) when Spitz's sharp teeth scored his flank. But no matter how Spitz circled, Joe whirled around on his heels to face him, mane bristling, ears laid back, lips writhing and snarling, jaws clipping together as fast as he could snap, and eyes diabolically gleaming—the incarnation of belligerent fear. So terrible was his appearance that Spitz was forced to forego disciplining him; but to cover his own discomfiture he turned upon the inoffensive and wailing Billee and drove him to the confines of the camp.

By evening Perrault secured another dog, an old husky, long and lean and gaunt, with a battle-scarred face and a single eye which flashed a warning of prowess that commanded respect. He was called Sol-leks, which means the Angry One. Like Dave, he asked nothing, gave nothing, expected nothing: and when he marched slowly and deliberately into their midst, even Spitz left him alone. He had one peculiarity which Buck was unlucky enough to discover. He did not like to be approached on his blind side. Of this offence Buck was unwittingly guilty, and the first knowledge he had of his indiscretion was when Sol-leks whirled upon him and slashed his shoulder to the bone for three inches up and down. Forever after Buck avoided his blind side, and to the last of their comradeship had no more trouble. His only apparent ambition, like Dave's, was to be left alone, though, as Buck was afterward to learn,[7] each of them possessed one other and even more vital ambition.

That night Buck faced the great problem of sleeping. The tent, illuminated by a candle, glowed warmly in the midst of the white plain; and when he, as a matter of course, entered it, both Perrault and François bombarded him with curses and cooking utensils, till he recovered from his consternation and fled ignominiously into the outer cold. A chill wind was blowing that nipped him sharply and bit with especial venom into his wounded shoulder. He lay down on the snow and attempted to sleep, but the frost soon drove him shivering to his feet. Miserable and disconsolate, he wandered about among the many tents, only to find that one place was as cold as another. Here and there savage dogs rushed upon him, but he bristled his neck-hair and snarled (for he was learning fast), and they let him go his way unmolested.

Finally an idea came to him. He would return and see how his own team mates were making out. To his astonishment, they had disappeared. Again he wandered about through the great camp, looking for them, and again he returned. Were they in the tent? No, that could not be, else he would not have been driven out. Then where could they possibly be? With drooping tail and shivering body, very forlorn indeed, he aimlessly circled the tent. Suddenly the snow gave way beneath his fore legs and he sank down. Something wriggled under his feet. He sprang back, bristling and snarling, fearful of the unseen and unknown. But a friendly little yelp reassured him, and he went back to investigate. A whiff of warm air ascended to his nostrils, and there, curled up under the snow in a snug ball, lay Billee. He whined placatingly, squirmed and wriggled to show his good will and intentions, and even ventured, as a bribe for peace, to lick Buck's face with his warm wet tongue.

Another lesson. So that was the way they did it, eh? Buck confidently selected a spot, and with much fuss and waste effort proceeded to dig a hole for himself. In a trice the heat from his body filled the confined space and he was asleep. The day had been long and arduous, and he slept soundly and comfortably, though he growled and barked and wrestled with bad dreams.

Nor did he open his eyes till roused by the noises of the waking camp. At first he did not know where he was. It had snowed during the night and he was completely buried. The snow walls pressed him on every side, and a great surge of fear swept through him—the fear of the wild thing for the trap. It was a token that he was harking back through his own life to the lives of his forebears, for he was a civilized dog, an unduly civilized dog and of his own experience knew no trap and so could not of himself fear it. The muscles of his whole body contracted spasmodically and instinctively, the hair on his neck and shoulders stood on end, and with a ferocious snarl he bounded straight up into the blinding day, the snow flying about him in a flashing cloud. Ere he landed on his feet, he saw the white camp spread out before him and knew where he was and remembered all that had passed from the time he went for a stroll with Manuel to the hole he had dug for himself the night before.

A shout from François hailed his appearance. "Wot I

say?" the dog driver cried to Perrault. "Dat Buck for sure learn queek as anyt'ing."

Perrault nodded gravely. As courier for the Canadian Government, bearing important despatches, he was anxious to secure the best dogs, and he was particularly gladdened by the possession of Buck.

Three more huskies were added to the team inside an hour, making a total of nine, and before another quarter of an hour had passed they were in harness and swinging up the trail toward the Dyea Cañon. Buck was glad to be gone, and though the work was hard he found he did not particularly despise it. He was surprised at the eagerness which animated the whole team and which was communicated to him; but still more surprising was the change wrought in Dave and Sol-leks. They were new dogs, utterly transformed by the harness. All passiveness and unconcern had dropped from them. They were alert and active, anxious that the work should go well, and fiercely irritable with whatever, by delay or confusion, retarded that work. The toil of the traces seemed the supreme expression of their being, and all that they lived for and the only thing in which they took delight.

Dave was wheeler or sled dog, pulling in front of him was Buck, then came Sol-leks; the rest of the team was strung out ahead, single file, to the leader, which position was filled by Spitz.

Buck had been purposely placed between Dave and Sol-leks so that he might receive instruction. Apt scholar that he was, they were equally apt teachers, never allowing him to linger long in error, and enforcing their teaching with their sharp teeth. Dave was fair and very wise. He never nipped Buck without cause, and he never failed to nip him when he stood in need of it. As François's whip backed him up, Buck found it to be cheaper to mend his ways than to retaliate. Once, during a brief halt, when he got tangled in the traces and delayed the start, both Dave and Sol-leks flew at him and administered a sound trouncing. The resulting tangle was even worse, but Buck took good care to keep the traces clear thereafter; and ere the day was done, so well had he mastered his work, his mates about ceased nagging him. François's whip snapped less frequently, and Perrault even honored Buck by lifting up his feet and carefully examining them.

It was a hard day's run, up the cañon, through Sheep Camp, past the Scales and the timber line, across glaciers and snowdrifts hundreds of feet deep, and over the great Chilkoot Divide, which stands between the salt water and the fresh and guards forbiddingly the sad and lonely North. They made good time down the chain of lakes which fills the craters of extinct volcanoes, and late that night pulled into the huge camp at the head of Lake Bennett, where thousands of goldseekers were building boats against the breakup of the ice in the spring. Buck made his hole in the snow and slept the sleep of the exhausted just, but all too early was routed out in the cold darkness and harnessed with his mates to the sled.

That day they made forty miles, the trail being packed; but the next day, and for many days to follow, they broke their own trail, worked harder, and made poorer time. As a rule, Perrault travelled ahead of the team, packing the snow with webbed shoes to make it easier for them. François, guiding the sled at the gee-pole, sometimes exchanged places with him but not often. Perrault was in a hurry, and he prided himself on his knowledge of ice, which knowledge was indispensable, for the fall ice was very thin, and where there was swift water, there was no ice at all.

Day after day, for days unending, Buck toiled in the traces. Always, they broke camp in the dark, and the first gray of dawn found them hitting the trail with fresh miles reeled off behind them. And always they pitched camp after dark, eating their bit of fish, and crawling to sleep into the snow. Buck was ravenous. The pound and a half of sun-dried salmon, which was his ration for each day, seemed to go nowhere. He never had enough, and suffered from perpetual hunger pangs. Yet the other dogs, because they weighed less and were born to the life, received a pound only of the fish and managed to keep in good condition.

He swiftly lost the fastidiousness which had characterized his old life. A dainty eater, he found that his mates, finishing first, robbed him of his unfinished ration. There was no defending it. While he was fighting off two or three, it was disappearing down the throats of the others. To remedy this, he ate as fast as they; and, so greatly did hunger compel him, he was not above taking what did not belong to him. He watched and learned. When he saw Pike, one of the new dogs, a clever malingerer and thief, slyly steal a slice of bacon when Perrault's back was turned, he duplicated the performance the following day, getting away with the whole chunk. A great uproar was raised, but he was unsuspected, while

Dub, an awkward blunderer who was always getting caught, was punished for Buck's misdeed.

This first theft marked Buck as fit to survive in the hostile Northland environment. It marked his adaptability, his capacity to adjust himself to changing conditions, the lack of which would have meant swift and terrible death. It marked, further, the decay or going to pieces of his moral nature, a vain thing and a handicap in the ruthless struggle for existence. It was all well enough in the Southland, under the law of love and fellowship, to respect private property and personal feelings; but in the Northland, under the law of club and fang, whoso took such things into account was a fool, and in so far as he observed them he would fail to prosper.

Not that Buck reasoned it out. He was fit, that was all, and unconsciously he accommodated himself to the new mode of life. All his days, no matter what the odds, he had never run from a fight. But the club of the man in the red sweater had beaten into him a more fundamental and primitive code. Civilized, he could have died for a moral consideration, say the defence of Judge Miller's riding whip; but the completeness of his decivilization was now evidenced by his ability to flee from the defence of a moral consideration and so save his hide. He did not steal for joy of it, but because of the clamor of his stomach. He did not rob openly, but stole secretly and cunningly, out of respect for club and fang. In short, the things he did were done because it was easier to do them than not to do them.

His development (or retrogression) was rapid. His muscles became hard as iron and he grew callous to all ordinary pain. He achieved an internal as well as external economy. He could eat anything, no matter how loathsome or indigestible; and, once eaten, the juices of his stomach extracted the last least particle of nutriment; and his blood carried it to the farthest reaches of his body, building it into the toughest and stoutest of tissues. Sight and scent became remarkably keen, while his hearing developed such acuteness that in his sleep he heard the faintest sound and knew whether it heralded peace or peril. He learned to bite the ice out with his teeth when it collected between his toes; and when he was thirsty and there was a thick scum of ice over the water hole, he would break it by rearing and striking it with stiff fore legs. His most conspicuous trait was an ability to scent the wind and forecast it a night in advance. No matter how breathless the air when he dug his nest by tree or bank, the wind that later blew inevitably found him to leeward, sheltered and snug.

And not only did he learn by experience, but instincts long dead became alive again. The domesticated generations fell from him. In vague ways he remembered back to the youth of the breed, to the time the wild dogs ranged in packs through the primeval forest, and killed their meat as they ran it down. It was no task for him to learn to fight with cut and slash and the quick wolf snap. In this manner had fought forgotten ancestors. They quickened the old life within him, and the old tricks which they had stamped into the heredity of the breed were his tricks. They came to him without effort or discovery, as though they had been his always. And when, on the still cold nights, he pointed his nose at a star and howled long and wolflike, it was his ancestors, dead and dust, pointing nose at star and howling down through the centuries and through him. And his cadences were their cadences, the cadences which voiced their woe and what to them was the meaning of the stillness, and the cold, and dark.

Thus, as token of what a puppet thing life is the ancient song surged through him and he came into his own again; and he came because men had found a yellow metal in the North, and because Manuel was a gardener's helper whose wages did not lap over the needs of his wife and divers small copies of himself.

Why he is here and how his wolf like ansestors come out during his stay in the Tundr

3

THE DOMINANT PRIMORDIAL BEAST

The dominant primordial beast was strong in Buck, and under the fierce conditions of trail life it grew and grew. Yet it was a secret growth. His new-born cunning gave him poise and control. He was too busy adjusting himself to the new life to feel at ease, and not only did he not pick fights, but he avoided them whenever possible. A certain deliberateness characterized his attitude. He was not prone to rashness and precipitate action; and in the bitter hatred between him and Spitz he betrayed no impatience, shunned all offensive acts.

On the other hand, possibly because he divined in Buck a dangerous rival, Spitz never lost an opportunity of showing his teeth. He even went out of his way to bully Buck, striving constantly to start the fight which could end only in the death of one or the other.

Early in the trip this might have taken place had it not been for an unwonted accident. At the end of this day they made a bleak and miserable camp on the shore of Lake Le Barge. Driving snow, a wind that cut like a white-hot knife, and darkness, had forced them to grope for a camping place. They could hardly have fared worse. At their backs rose a perpendicular wall of rock, and Perrault and François were compelled to make their fire and spread their sleeping robes on the ice of the lake itself. The tent they had discarded at Dyea in order to travel light. A few sticks of driftwood furnished them with a fire that thawed down through the ice and left them to eat supper in the dark.

Close in under the sheltering rock Buck made his nest. So snug and warm was it, that he was loath to leave it when François distributed the fish which he had first thawed over the fire. But when Buck finished his ration and returned, he found his nest occupied. A warning snarl told him that the trespasser was Spitz. Till now Buck had avoided trouble with his enemy, but this was too much. The beast in him roared. He sprang upon Spitz with a fury which surprised them both, and Spitz particularly, for his whole experience with Buck had gone to teach him that his rival was an unusually timid dog, who managed to hold his own only because of his great weight and size.

François was surprised, too, when they shot out in a tangle from the disrupted nest and he divined the cause of the trouble. "A-a-ah!" he cried to Buck. "Gif it to heem, by Gar! Gif it to heem, the dirty t'eef!"

Spitz was equally willing. He was crying with sheer rage and eagerness as he circled back and forth for a chance to spring in. Buck was no less eager, and no less cautious, as he likewise circled back and forth for the advantage. But it was then that the unexpected happened, the thing which projected their struggle for su-

premacy far into the future, past many a weary mile of
trail and toil.

An oath from Perrault, the resounding impact of a
club upon a bony frame, and a shrill yelp of pain, heralded the breaking forth of pandemonium. The camp
was suddenly discovered to be alive with skulking furry
forms,—starving huskies, four or five score of them,
who had scented the camp from some Indian village.
They had crept in while Buck and Spitz were fighting,
and when the two men sprang among them with stout
clubs they showed their teeth and fought back. They
were crazed by the smell of the food. Perrault found
one with head buried in the grub-box. His club landed
heavily on the gaunt ribs, and the grub-box was capsized
on the ground. On the instant a score of the famished
brutes were scrambling for the bread and bacon. The
clubs fell upon them unheeded. They yelped and
howled under the rain of blows, but struggled none the
less madly till the last crumb had been devoured.

In the meantime the astonished team-dogs had burst
out of their nests only to be set upon by the fierce in-
vaders. Never had Buck seen such dogs. It seemed as
though their bones would burst through their skins.
They were mere skeletons, draped loosely in draggled
hides, with blazing eyes and slavered fangs. But the
hunger-madness made them terrifying, irresistible.
There was no opposing them. The team-dogs were
swept back against the cliff at the first onset. Buck was
beset by three huskies, and in a trice his head and shoulders were ripped and slashed. The din was frightful.
Billee was crying as usual. Dave and Sol-leks, dripping

blood from a score of wounds, were fighting bravely side by side. Joe was snapping like a demon. Once, his teeth closed on the fore leg of a husky, and he crunched down through the bone. Pike, the malingerer, leaped upon the crippled animal, breaking its neck with a quick dash of teeth and a jerk. Buck got a frothing adversary by the throat, and was sprayed with blood when his teeth sank through the jugular. The warm taste of it in his mouth goaded him to greater fierceness. He flung himself upon another, and at the same time felt teeth sink into his own throat. It was Spitz treacherously attacking from the side.

Perrault and François, having cleaned out their part of the camp, hurried to save their sled-dogs. The wild wave of famished beasts rolled back before them, and Buck shook himself free. But it was only for a moment. The two men were compelled to run back to save the grub, upon which the huskies returned to the attack on the team. Billee, terrified into bravery, sprang through the savage circle and fled away over the ice. Pike and Dub followed on his heels, with the rest of the team behind. As Buck drew himself together to spring after them, out of the tail of his eye he saw Spitz rush upon him with the evident intention of overthrowing him. Once off his feet and under that mass of huskies, there was no hope for him. But he braced himself to the shock of Spitz's charge, then joined the flight out on the lake.

Later, the nine team-dogs gathered together and sought shelter in the forest. Though unpursued, they were in a sorry plight. There was not one who was not wounded in four or five places, while some were wounded grievously. Dub was badly injured in a hind leg; Dolly, the last husky added to the team at Dyea, had a badly torn throat; Joe had lost an eye; while Billee, the good-natured, with an ear chewed and rent to ribbons, cried and whimpered throughout the night. At daybreak they limped warily back to camp, to find the marauders gone and the two men in bad tempers. Fully half their grub supply was gone. The huskies had chewed through the sled lashings and canvas coverings. In fact, nothing, no matter how remotely eatable, had escaped them. They had eaten a pair of Perrault's moose-hide moccasins, chunks out of the leather traces, and even two feet of lash from the end of François's whip. He broke from a mournful contemplation of it to look over his wounded dogs.

"Ah, my frien's," he said softly, "mebbe it mek you mad dog, dose many bites. Mebbe all mad dog, sacredam! Wot you t'ink, eh, Perrault?"

The courier shook his head dubiously. With four hundred miles of trail still between him and Dawson, he could ill afford to have madness break out among his dogs. Two hours of cursing and exertion got the harnesses into shape, and the wound-stiffened team was under way, struggling painfully over the hardest part of the trail they had yet encountered, and for that matter, the hardest between them and Dawson.

The Thirty Mile River was wide open. Its wild water defied the frost, and it was in the eddies only and in the quiet places that the ice held at all. Six days of exhausting toil were required to cover those thirty terrible miles. And terrible they were, for every foot of them

was accomplished at the risk of life to dog and man. A
dozen times, Perrault, nosing the way, broke through
the ice bridges, being saved by the long pole he carried,
which he so held that it fell each time across the hole
made by his body. But a cold snap was on, the ther-
mometer registering fifty below zero, and each time he
broke through he was compelled for very life to build a
fire and dry his garments.

Nothing daunted him. It was because nothing
daunted him that he had been chosen for government
courier. He took all manner of risks, resolutely thrusting
his little weazened face into the frost and struggling on
from dim dawn to dark. He skirted the frowning shores
on rim ice that bent and crackled under foot and on
which they dared not halt. Once, the sled broke
through, with Dave and Buck, and they were half-
frozen and all but drowned by the time they were
dragged out. The usual fire was necessary to save them.
They were coated solidly with ice, and the two men kept
them on the run around the fire, sweating and thawing,
so close that they were singed by the flames.

At another time Spitz went through, dragging the
whole team after him up to Buck, who strained backward
with all his strength, his fore paws on the slippery edge
and the ice quivering and snapping all around. But behind
him was Dave, likewise straining backward, and behind
the sled was François, pulling till his tendons cracked.

Again, the rim ice broke away before and behind,
and there was no escape except up the cliff. Perrault
scaled it by a miracle, while François prayed for just
that miracle; and with every thong and sled-lashing and

the last bit of harness rove into a long rope, the dogs were hoisted, one by one, to the cliff crest. François came up last, after the sled and load. Then came the search for a place to descend, which descent was ultimately made by the aid of the rope, and night found them back on the river with a quarter of a mile to the day's credit.

By the time they made the Houtalinqua and good ice, Buck was played out. The rest of the dogs were in like condition; but Perrault, to make up lost time, pushed them late and early. The first day they covered thirty-five miles to the Big Salmon; the next day thirty-five more to the Little Salmon; the third day forty miles, which brought them well up toward the Five Fingers.

Buck's feet were not so compact and hard as the feet of the huskies. His had softened during the many generations since the day his last wild ancestor was tamed by a cave-dweller or river man. All day long he limped in agony, and camp once made, lay down like a dead dog. Hungry as he was, he would not move to receive his ration of fish, which François had to bring to him. Also, the dog-driver rubbed Buck's feet for half an hour each night after supper, and sacrificed the tops of his own moccasins to make four moccasins for Buck. This was a great relief, and Buck caused even the weazened face of Perrault to twist itself into a grin one morning, when François forgot the moccasins and Buck lay on his back, his four feet waving appealingly in the air, and refused to budge without them. Later his feet grew hard to the trail, and the worn-out footgear was thrown away.

At the Pelly one morning, as they were harnessing

up, Dolly, who had never been conspicuous for anything, went suddenly mad. She announced her condition by a long, heartbreaking wolf howl that sent every
dog bristling with fear, then sprang straight for Buck.
He had never seen a dog go mad, nor did he have any
reason to fear madness; yet he knew that here was hor-
ror, and fled away from it in panic. Straight away he
raced, with Dolly, panting and frothing, one leap behind; nor could she gain on him, so great was his terror,
nor could he leave her, so great was her madness. He
plunged through the wooded breast of the island, flew
down to the lower end, crossed a back channel filled
with rough ice to another island, gained a third island,
curved back to the main river, and in desperation
started to cross it. And all the time, though he did not
look, he could hear her snarling just one leap behind.
François called to him a quarter of a mile away and he
doubled back, still one leap ahead, gasping painfully for
air and putting all his faith in that François would save
him. The dog-driver held the axe poised in his hand,
and as Buck shot past him the axe crashed down upon
mad Dolly's head.

Buck staggered over against the sled, exhausted, sobbing for breath, helpless. This was Spitz's opportunity.
He sprang upon Buck, and twice his teeth sank into his
unresisting foe and ripped and tore the flesh to the
bone. Then François's lash descended, and Buck had
the satisfaction of watching Spitz receive the worst
whipping as yet administered to any of the team.

"One devil, dat Spitz," remarked Perrault. "Some
dam day heem keel dat Buck."

"Dat Buck two devils," was François's rejoinder. "All de tam I watch dat Buck I know for sure. Lissen: some dam fine day heem get mad lak hell an' den heem chew dat Spitz all up an' spit heem out on de snow. Sure. I know."

From then on it was war between them. Spitz, as lead-dog and acknowledged master of the team, felt his supremacy threatened by this strange Southland dog. And strange Buck was to him, for of the many Southland dogs he had known, not one had shown up worthily in camp and on the trail. They were all too soft, dying under the toil, the frost, and starvation. Buck was the exception. He alone endured and prospered, matching the husky in strength, savagery, and cunning. Then he was a masterful dog, and what made him dangerous was the fact that the club of the man in the red sweater had knocked all blind pluck and rashness out of his desire for mastery. He was preëminently cunning, and could bide his time with a patience that was nothing less than primitive.

It was inevitable that the clash for leadership should come. Buck wanted it. He wanted it because it was his nature, because he had been gripped tight by that nameless, incomprehensible pride of the trail and trace—that pride which holds dogs in the toil to the last gasp, which lures them to die joyfully in the harness, and breaks their hearts if they are cut out of the harness. This was the pride of Dave as wheel-dog, of Sol-leks as he pulled with all his strength; the pride that laid hold of them at break of camp, transforming them from sour and sullen brutes into straining, eager, ambitious creatures; the pride that spurred them on all day and dropped them at pitch of camp at night, letting them fall into gloomy unrest and uncontent. This was the pride that bore up Spitz and made him thrash the sled-dogs who blundered and shirked in the traces or hid away at harness-up time in the morning. Likewise it was this pride that made him fear Buck as a possible lead-dog. And this was Buck's pride, too.

He openly threatened the other's leadership. He came between him and the shirks he should have punished. And he did it deliberately. One night there was a heavy snowfall, and in the morning Pike, the malingerer, did not appear. He was securely hidden in his nest under a foot of snow. François called him and sought him in vain. Spitz was wild with wrath. He raged through the camp, smelling and digging in every likely place, snarling so frightfully that Pike heard and shivered in his hiding-place.

But when he was at last unearthed, and Spitz flew at him to punish him, Buck flew, with equal rage, in between. So unexpected was it, and so shrewdly managed, that Spitz was hurled backward and off his feet. Pike, who had been trembling abjectly, took heart at this open mutiny, and sprang upon his overthrown leader. Buck, to whom fairplay was a forgotten code, likewise sprang upon Spitz. But François, chuckling at the incident while unswerving in the administration of justice, brought his lash down upon Buck with all his might. This failed to drive Buck from his prostrate rival, and the butt of the whip was brought into play. Half-stunned by the blow, Buck was knocked backward and the lash laid upon him again and again, while Spitz soundly punished the many times offending Pike.

In the days that followed, as Dawson grew closer and closer, Buck still continued to interfere between Spitz and the culprits; but he did it craftily, when François was not around. With the covert mutiny of Buck, a general insubordination sprang up and increased. Dave and Sol-leks were unaffected, but the rest of the team went from bad to worse. Things no longer went right. There was continual bickering and jangling. Trouble was always afoot, and at the bottom of it was Buck. He kept François busy, for the dog-driver was in constant apprehension of the life-and-death struggle between the two which he knew must take place sooner or later; and on more than one night the sounds of quarrelling and strife among the other dogs turned him out of his sleeping robe, fearful that Buck and Spitz were at it.

But the opportunity did not present itself, and they pulled into Dawson one dreary afternoon with the great fight still to come. Here were many men, and countless dogs, and Buck found them all at work. It seemed the ordained order of things that dogs should work. All day they swung up and down the main street in long teams, and in the night their jingling bells still went by. They hauled cabin logs and firewood, freighted up to the mines, and did all manner of work that horses did in the Santa Clara Valley. Here and there Buck met Southland dogs, but in the main they were the wild wolf husky breed. Every night, regularly, at nine, at twelve, at three, they lifted a nocturnal song, a weird and eerie chant, in which it was Buck's delight to join.

With the aurora borealis flaming coldly overhead, or the stars leaping in the frost dance, and the land numb and frozen under its pall of snow, this song of the huskies might have been the defiance of life, only it was pitched in minor key, with long-drawn wailings and half-sobs, and was more the pleading of life, the articulate travail of existence. It was an old song, old as the breed itself—one of the first songs of the younger world in a day when songs were sad. It was invested with the woe of unnumbered generations, this plaint by which Buck was so strangely stirred. When he moaned and sobbed, it was with the pain of living that was of old the pain of his wild fathers, and the fear and mystery of the cold and dark that was to them fear and mystery. And that he should be stirred by it marked the completeness with which he harked back through the ages of fire and roof to the raw beginnings of life in the howling ages.

Seven days from the time they pulled into Dawson, they dropped down the steep bank by the Barracks to the Yukon Trail, and pulled for Dyea and Salt Water. Perrault was carrying despatches if anything more urgent than those he had brought in; also, the travel pride had gripped him, and he purposed to make the record trip of the year. Several things favored him in this. The week's rest had recuperated the dogs and put them in thorough trim. The trail they had broken into the country was packed hard by later journeyers. And further, the police had arranged in two or three places deposits of grub for dog and man, and he was travelling light.

They made Sixty Miles, which is a fifty-mile run, on the first day; and the second day saw them booming up the Yukon well on their way to Pelly. But such splendid running was achieved not without great trouble and vexation on the part of François. The insidious revolt led by Buck had destroyed the solidarity of the team. It no longer was as one dog leaping in the traces. The encouragement Buck gave the rebels led them into all kinds of petty misdemeanors. No more was Spitz a leader greatly to be feared. The old awe departed, and they grew equal to challenging his authority. Pike robbed him of half a fish one night, and gulped it down under the protection of Buck. Another night Dub and Joe fought Spitz and made him forego the punishment they deserved. And even Billee, the good-natured, was less good-natured, and whined not half so placatingly as in former days. Buck never came near Spitz without snarling and bristling menacingly. In fact, his conduct approached that of a bully, and he was given to swaggering up and down before Spitz's very nose.

The breaking down of discipline likewise affected the dogs in their relations with one another. They quarrelled and bickered more than ever among themselves, till at times the camp was a howling bedlam. Dave and Sol-leks alone were unaltered, though they were made irritable by the unending squabbling. François swore strange barbarous oaths, and stamped the snow in futile rage, and tore his hair. His lash was always singing among the dogs, but it was of small avail. Directly his back was turned they were at it again. He backed up Spitz with his whip, while Buck backed up the remainder of the team. François knew he was behind all the trouble, and Buck knew he knew; but Buck was too clever ever again to be caught red-handed. He worked faithfully in the harness, for the toil had become a delight to him; yet it was a greater delight slyly to precipitate a fight amongst his mates and tangle the traces.

At the mouth of the Tahkeena, one night after supper, Dub turned up a snowshoe rabbit, blundered it, and missed. In a second the whole team was in full cry. A hundred yards away was a camp of the Northwest Police,[8] with fifty dogs, huskies all, who joined the chase. The rabbit sped down the river, turned off into a small creek, up the frozen bed of which it held steadily. It ran lightly on the surface of the snow, while the dogs ploughed through by main strength. Buck led the pack, sixty strong, around bend after bend, but he could not gain. He lay down low to the race, whining eagerly, his splendid body flashing forward, leap by leap, in the wan white moonlight. And leap by leap, like some pale frost wraith, the snowshoe rabbit flashed on ahead.

All that stirring of old instincts which at stated periods drives men out from the sounding cities to forest and plain to kill things by chemically propelled leaden pellets, the blood lust, the joy to kill—all this was Buck's, only it was infinitely more intimate. He was ranging at the head of the pack, running the wild thing down, the living meat, to kill with his own teeth and wash his muzzle to the eyes in warm blood.

There is an ecstasy that marks the summit of life, and beyond which life cannot rise. And such is the paradox of living, this ecstasy comes when one is most alive, and it comes as a complete forgetfulness that one is alive. This ecstasy, this forgetfulness of living, comes to the artist, caught up and out of himself in a sheet of flame; it comes to the soldier, war-mad on a stricken field and refusing quarter; and it came to Buck, leading the pack, sounding the old wolf-cry, straining after the food that was alive and that fled swiftly before him through the moonlight. He was sounding the deeps of his nature, and of the parts of his nature that were deeper than he, going back into the womb of Time. He was mastered by the sheer surging of life, the tidal wave of being, the perfect joy of each separate muscle, joint, and sinew and that it was everything that was not death, that it was aglow and rampant, expressing itself in movement, flying exultantly under the stars and over the face of dead matter that did not move.

But Spitz, cold and calculating even in his supreme moods, left the pack and cut across a narrow neck of land where the creek made a long bend around. Buck did not know of this, and as he rounded the bend, the frost wraith of a rabbit still flitting before him, he saw another and larger frost wraith leap from the overhanging bank into the immediate path of the rabbit. It was Spitz. The rabbit could not turn, and as the white teeth broke its back in mid air it shrieked as loudly as a stricken man may shriek. At sound of this, the cry of Life plunging down from Life's apex in the grip of Death, the full pack at Buck's heels raised a hell's chorus of delight.

Buck did not cry out. He did not check himself, but drove in upon Spitz, shoulder to shoulder, so hard that he missed the throat. They rolled over and over in the powdery snow. Spitz gained his feet almost as though he had not been overthrown, slashing Buck down the shoulder and leaping clear. Twice his teeth clipped together, like the steel jaws of a trap, as he backed away for better footing, with lean and lifting lips that writhed and snarled.

In a flash Buck knew it. The time had come. It was to the death. As they circled about, snarling, ears laid back, keenly watchful for the advantage, the scene came to Buck with a sense of familiarity. He seemed to remember it all,—the white woods, and earth, and moonlight, and the thrill of battle. Over the whiteness and silence brooded a ghostly calm. There was not the faintest whisper of air[9]—nothing moved, not a leaf quivered, the visible breaths of the dogs rising slowly and lingering in the frosty air. They had made short work of the snowshoe rabbit, these dogs that were ill-tamed wolves; and they were now drawn up in an expectant circle. They, too, were silent, their eyes only gleaming and their breaths drifting slowly upward. To Buck it was nothing new or strange, this scene of old time. It was as though it had always been, the wonted way of things.

Spitz was a practised fighter. From Spitzbergen through the Arctic, and across Canada and the Barrens, he had held his own with all manner of dogs and achieved to mastery over them. Bitter rage was his, but never blind rage. In passion to rend and destroy, he never forgot that his enemy was in like passion to rend and destroy. He never rushed till he was prepared to receive a rush; never attacked till he had first defended that attack.

In vain Buck strove to sink his teeth in the neck of the big white dog. Wherever his fangs struck for the softer flesh, they were countered by the fangs of Spitz. Fang clashed fang, and lips were cut and bleeding, but Buck could not penetrate his enemy's guard. Then he

warmed up and enveloped Spitz in a whirlwind of
rushes. Time and time again he tried for the snow-white
throat, where life bubbled near to the surface, and each
time and every time Spitz slashed him and got away.
Then Buck took to rushing, as though for the throat,
when, suddenly drawing back his head and curving in
from the side, he would drive his shoulder at the shoulder of Spitz, as a ram by which to overthrow him. But
instead, Buck's shoulder was slashed down each time as
Spitz leaped lightly away.

Spitz was untouched, while Buck was streaming with
blood and panting hard. The fight was growing desperate. And all the while the silent and wolfish circle waited
to finish off whichever dog went down. As Buck grew
winded, Spitz took to rushing, and he kept him staggering for footing. Once Buck went over, and the whole circle of sixty dogs started up; but he recovered himself,
almost in mid air, and the circle sank down again and
waited.

But Buck possessed a quality that made for great-
ness—imagination. He fought by instinct, but he could
fight by head as well. He rushed, as though attempting
the old shoulder trick, but at the last instant swept low
to the snow and in. His teeth closed on Spitz's left fore
leg. There was a crunch of breaking bone, and the white
dog faced him on three legs. Thrice he tried to knock
him over, then repeated the trick and broke the right
fore leg. Despite the pain and helplessness, Spitz struggled madly to keep up. He saw the silent circle, with
gleaming eyes, lolling tongues, and silvery breaths drifting upward, closing in upon him as he had seen similar

circles close in upon beaten antagonists in the past. Only this time he was the one who was beaten.

There was no hope for him. Buck was inexorable. Mercy was a thing reserved for gentler climes. He manœuvred for the final rush. The circle had tightened till he could feel the breaths of the huskies on his flanks. He could see them, beyond Spitz and to either side, half crouching for the spring, their eyes fixed upon him. A pause seemed to fall. Every animal was motionless as though turned to stone. Only Spitz quivered and bristled as he staggered back and forth, snarling with horrible menace, as though to frighten off impending death. Then Buck sprang in and out, but while he was in, shoulder had at last squarely met shoulder. The dark circle became a dot on the moon-flooded snow as Spitz disappeared from view. Buck stood and looked on, the successful champion, the dominant primordial beast who had made his kill and found it good.

4

WHO HAS WON
TO MASTERSHIP

"Eh? Wot I say? I spik true w'en I say dat Buck two devils."

This was François's speech next morning when he discovered Spitz missing and Buck covered with wounds. He drew him to the fire and by its light pointed them out.

"Dat Spitz fight lak hell," said Perrault, as he surveyed the gaping rips and cuts.

"An' dat Buck fight lak two hells," was François's answer. "An' now we make good time. No more Spitz, no more trouble, sure."

While Perrault packed the camp outfit and loaded the sled, the dog-driver proceeded to harness the dogs. Buck trotted up to the place Spitz would have occupied as leader; but François, not noticing him, brought Sol-leks to the coveted position. In his judgment, Sol-leks was the best lead-dog left. Buck sprang upon Sol-leks in a fury, driving him back and standing in his place.

"Eh? eh?" François cried, slapping his thighs gleefully. "Look at dat Buck. Heem keel dat Spitz, heem t'ink to take de job."

"Go 'way, Chook!" he cried, but Buck refused to budge.

He took Buck by the scruff of the neck, and though the dog growled threateningly, dragged him to one side and replaced Sol-leks. The old dog did not like it, and showed plainly that he was afraid of Buck. François was obdurate, but when he turned his back Buck again displaced Sol-leks, who was not at all unwilling to go.

François was angry. "Now, by Gar, I feex you!" he cried, coming back with a heavy club in his hand.

Buck remembered the man in the red sweater, and retreated slowly; nor did he attempt to charge in when Sol-leks was once more brought forward. But he circled just beyond the range of the club, snarling with bitterness and rage; and while he circled he watched the club so as to dodge it if thrown by François, for he was become wise in the way of clubs.

The driver went about his work, and he called to Buck when he was ready to put him in his old place in front of Dave. Buck retreated two or three steps. François followed him up, whereupon he again retreated. After some time of this, François threw down the club, thinking that Buck feared a thrashing. But Buck was in open revolt. He wanted, not to escape a clubbing, but to have the leadership. It was his by right. He had earned it, and he would not be content with less.

Perrault took a hand. Between them they ran him about the better part of an hour. They threw clubs at him. He dodged. They cursed him, and his fathers and mothers before him, and all his seed to come after him down to the remotest generation, and every hair on his body and drop of blood in his veins; and he answered curse with snarl and kept out of their reach. He did not try to run away, but retreated around and around the camp, advertising plainly that when his desire was met, he would come in and be good.

François sat down and scratched his head. Perrault looked at his watch and swore. Time was flying, and they should have been on the trail an hour gone. François scratched his head again. He shook it and grinned sheepishly at the courier, who shrugged his shoulders in sign that they were beaten. Then François went up to where Sol-leks stood and called to Buck. Buck laughed, as dogs laugh, yet kept his distance. François unfastened Sol-leks's traces and put him back in his old place. The team stood harnessed to the sled in an unbroken line, ready for the trail. There was no place for Buck save at the front. Once more François called, and once more Buck laughed and kept away.

"T'row down de club," Perrault commanded.

François complied, whereupon Buck trotted in, laughing triumphantly, and swung around into position at the head of the team. His traces were fastened, the sled broken out, and with both men running they dashed out on to the river trail.

Highly as the dog-driver had forevalued Buck, with his two devils, he found, while the day was yet young, that he had undervalued. At a bound Buck took up the duties of leadership; and where judgment was required, and quick thinking and quick acting, he showed himself the superior even of Spitz, of whom François had never seen an equal.

But it was in giving the law and making his mates live up to it, that Buck excelled. Dave and Sol-leks did not mind the change in leadership. It was none of their business. Their business was to toil, and toil mightily, in the traces. So long as that were not interfered with, they did not care what happened. Billee, the good-natured, could lead for all they cared so long as he kept order. The rest of the team, however, had grown unruly during the last days of Spitz, and their surprise was great now that Buck proceeded to lick them into shape.

Pike, who pulled at Buck's heels, and who never put an ounce more of his weight against the breast band than he was compelled to do, was swiftly and repeatedly shaken for loafing, and ere the first day was done he was pulling more than ever before in his life. The first night in camp, Joe, the sour one, was punished roundly—a thing that Spitz had never succeeded in doing. Buck simply smothered him by virtue of superior weight, and cut him up till he ceased snapping and began to whine for mercy.

The general tone of the team picked up immediately. It recovered its old-time solidarity, and once more the dogs leaped as one dog in the traces. At the Rink Rapids two native huskies, Teek and Koona, were added; and the celerity with which Buck broke them in took away François's breath.

"Nevaire such a dog as dat Buck!" he cried. "No, nevaire! Heem worth one t'ousan' dollair, by Gar! Eh? Wot you say, Perrault?"

And Perrault nodded. He was ahead of the record then, and gaining day by day. The trail was in excellent condition, well packed and hard, and there was no new-fallen snow with which to contend. It was not too cold. The temperature dropped to fifty below zero and remained there the whole trip. The men rode and ran by turn, and the dogs were kept on the jump, with but infrequent stoppages.

The Thirty Mile River was comparatively coated with ice, and they covered in one day going out what had taken them ten days coming in. In one run they made a sixty-mile dash from the foot of Lake Le Barge to the White Horse Rapids. Across Marsh, Tagish, and Bennett (seventy miles of lakes), they flew so fast that the man whose turn it was to run towed behind the sled at the end of a rope. And on the last night of the second week they topped White Pass and dropped down the sea slope with the lights of Skagway and of the shipping at their feet.

It was a record run. Each day for fourteen days they had averaged forty miles. For three days Perrault and François threw chests up and down the main street of Skagway and were deluged with invitations to drink, while the team was the constant centre of a worshipful crowd of dog-busters and mushers. Then three or four Western bad men aspired to clean out the town, were riddled like timber boxes for their pains, and public interest turned to other idols. Next came official orders. François called Buck to him, threw his arms around him, wept over him. And that was the last of François and Perrault. Like other men, they passed out of Buck's life for good.

A Scotch half-breed took charge of him and his mates, and in company with a dozen other dog-teams he started back over the weary trail to Dawson. It was no light running now, nor record time, but heavy toil each day, with a heavy load behind; for this was the mail train, carrying word from the world to the men who sought gold under the shadow of the Pole.

Buck did not like it, but he bore up well to the work, taking pride in it after the manner of Dave and Sol-leks, and seeing that his mates, whether they prided in it or not, did their fair share. It was a monotonous life, operating with machine-like regularity. One day was very like another. At a certain time each morning the cooks turned out, fires were built, and breakfast was eaten. Then while some broke camp, others harnessed the dogs, and they were under way an hour or so before the darkness which gave warning of dawn. At night, camp was made. Some pitched the flies, others cut firewood and pine boughs for the beds, and still others carried water or ice for the cooks. Also, the dogs were fed. To them, this was the one feature of the day, though it was good to loaf around, after the fish was eaten, for an hour or so with the other dogs, of which there were fivescore and odd. There were fierce fighters among them, but three battles with the fiercest brought Buck to mastery, so that when he bristled and showed his teeth they got out of his way.

Best of all, perhaps, he loved to lie near the fire, hind legs crouched under him, fore legs stretched out in front, head raised, and eyes blinking dreamily at the flames. Sometimes he thought of Judge Miller's big house in the sun-kissed Santa Clara Valley, and of the cement swimming-tank, and Ysabel, the Mexican hairless, and Toots, the Japanese pug; but oftener he remembered the man in the red sweater, the death of

Curly, the great fight with Spitz, and the good things he had eaten or would like to eat. He was not homesick. The Sunland was very dim and distant, and such memories had no power over him. Far more potent were the memories of his heredity that gave things he had never seen before a seeming familiarity; the instincts (which were but the memories of his ancestors become habits) which had lapsed in later days, and still later, in him, quickened and became alive again.

Sometimes as he crouched there, blinking dreamily at the flames, it seemed that the flames were of another fire, and that as he crouched by this other fire he saw another and different man from the half-breed cook before him. This other man was shorter of leg and longer of arm, with muscles that were stringy and knotty rather than rounded and swelling. The hair of this man was long and matted, and his head slanted back under it from the eyes. He uttered strange sounds, and seemed very much afraid of the darkness, into which he peered continually, clutching in his hand, which hung midway between knee and foot, a stick with a heavy stone made fast to the end. He was all but naked, a ragged and fire-scorched skin hanging part way down his back, but on his body there was much hair. In some places, across the chest and shoulders and down the outside of the arms and thighs, it was matted into almost a thick fur. He did not stand erect, but with trunk inclined forward from the hips, on legs that bent at the knees. About his body there was a peculiar springiness, or resiliency, almost catlike, and a quick alertness as of one who lived in perpetual fear of things seen and unseen.

At other times this hairy man squatted by the fire with head between his legs and slept. On such occasions his elbows were on his knees, his hands clasped above his head as though to shed rain by the hairy arms. And beyond that fire, in the circling darkness, Buck could see many gleaming coals, two by two, always two by two, which he knew to be the eyes of great beasts of prey. And he could hear the crashing of their bodies through the undergrowth, and the noises they made in the night. And dreaming there by the Yukon bank, with lazy eyes blinking at the fire, these sounds and sights of another world would make the hair to rise along his back and stand on end across his shoulders and up his neck, till he whimpered low and suppressedly, or growled softly, and the half-breed cook shouted at him, "Hey, you Buck, wake up!" Whereupon the other world would vanish and the real world come into his eyes, and he would get up and yawn and stretch as though he had been asleep.

It was a hard trip, with the mail behind them, and the heavy work wore them down. They were short of weight and in poor condition when they made Dawson, and should have had a ten days' or a week's rest at least. But in two days' time they dropped down the Yukon bank from the Barracks, loaded with letters for the outside. The dogs were tired, the drivers grumbling, and to make matters worse, it snowed every day. This meant a soft trail, greater friction on the runners, and heavier pulling for the dogs; yet the drivers were fair through it all, and did their best for the animals.

Each night the dogs were attended to first. They ate before the drivers ate, and no man sought his sleeping-robe till he had seen to the feet of the dogs he drove. Still, their strength went down. Since the beginning of the winter they had travelled eighteen hundred miles, dragging sleds the whole weary distance; and eighteen hundred miles will tell upon life of the toughest. Buck stood it, keeping his mates up to their work and maintaining discipline, though he too was very tired. Billee cried and whimpered regularly in his sleep each night. Joe was sourer than ever, and Sol-leks was unapproachable, blind side or other side.

But it was Dave who suffered most of all. Something had gone wrong with him. He became more morose and irritable, and when camp was pitched at once made his nest, where his driver fed him. Once out of the harness and down, he did not get on his feet again till harness-up time in the morning. Sometimes, in the traces, when jerked by a sudden stoppage of the sled, or by straining to start it, he would cry out with pain. The driver examined him, but could find nothing. All the drivers became interested in his case. They talked it over at mealtime, and over their last pipes before going to bed, and one night they held a consultation. He was brought from his nest to the fire and was pressed and prodded till he cried out many times. Something was wrong inside, but they could locate no broken bones, could not make it out.

By the time Cassiar Bar was reached, he was so weak that he was falling repeatedly in the traces. The Scotch half-breed called a halt and took him out of the team, making the next dog, Sol-leks, fast to the sled. His intention was to rest Dave, letting him run free behind the sled. Sick as he was, Dave resented being taken out, grunting and growling while the traces were unfastened, and whimpering broken-heartedly when he saw Sol-leks in the position he had held and served so long. For the pride of trace and trail was his, and sick unto death, he could not bear that another dog should do his work.

When the sled started, he floundered in the soft snow alongside the beaten trail, attacking Sol-leks with his teeth, rushing against him and trying to thrust him off into the soft snow on the other side, striving to leap inside his traces and get between him and the sled, and all the while whining and yelping and crying with grief and pain. The half-breed tried to drive him away with the whip; but he paid no heed to the stinging lash, and the man had not the heart to strike harder. Dave refused to run quietly on the trail behind the sled, where the going was easy, but continued to flounder alongside in the soft snow, where the going was most difficult, till exhausted, then he fell, and lay where he fell, howling lugubriously as the long train of sleds churned by.

With the last remnant of his strength he managed to stagger along behind till the train made another stop, when he floundered past the sleds to his own, where he stood alongside Sol-leks. His driver lingered a moment to get a light for his pipe from the man behind. Then he returned and started his dogs. They swung out on the trail with remarkable lack of exertion, turned their heads uneasily, and stopped in surprise. The driver was surprised, too; the sled had not moved. He called his comrades to witness the sight. Dave had bitten through both of Sol-leks's traces, and was standing directly in front of the sled in his proper place.

He pleaded with his eyes to remain there. The driver was perplexed. His comrades talked of how a dog could break its heart through being denied the work that killed it, and recalled instances they had known, where dogs, too old for the toil, or injured, had died because they were cut out of the traces. Also, they held it a mercy, since Dave was to die anyway, that he should die in the traces, heart-easy and content. So he was harnessed in again, and proudly he pulled as of old, though more than once he cried out involuntarily from the bite of his inward hurt. Several times he fell down and was dragged in the traces, and once the sled ran upon him so that he limped thereafter on one of his hind legs.

But he held out till camp was reached, when his driver made a place for him by the fire. Morning found him too weak to travel. At harness-up time he tried to crawl to his driver. By convulsive efforts he got on his feet, staggered, and fell. Then he wormed his way forward slowly toward where the harnesses were being put on his mates. He would advance his fore legs and drag up his body with a sort of hitching movement, when he would advance his fore legs and hitch ahead again for a few more inches. His strength left him, and the last his mates saw of him he lay gasping in the snow and yearning toward them. But they could hear him mournfully howling till they passed out of sight behind a belt of river timber.

Here the train was halted. The Scotch half-breed

slowly retraced his steps to the camp they had left. The men ceased talking. A revolver-shot rang out. The man came back hurriedly. The whips snapped, the bells tinkled merrily, the sleds churned along the trail; but Buck knew, and every dog knew, what had taken place behind the belt of river trees.

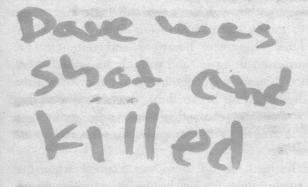

5

THE TOIL OF
TRACE AND TRAIL

Thirty days from the time it left Dawson, the Salt Water Mail, with Buck and his mates at the fore, arrived at Skagway. They were in a wretched state, worn out and worn down. Buck's one hundred and forty pounds had dwindled to one hundred and fifteen. The rest of his mates, though lighter dogs, had relatively lost more weight than he. Pike, the malingerer, who, in his life-time of deceit, had often successfully feigned a hurt leg, was now limping in earnest. Sol-leks was limping, and Dub was suffering from a wrenched shoulder blade.

They were all terribly footsore. No spring or rebound was left in them. Their feet fell heavily on the trail, jarring their bodies and doubling the fatigue of a day's travel. There was nothing the matter with them except that they were dead tired. It was not the dead-tiredness that comes through brief and excessive effort, from which recovery is a matter of hours; but it was the dead-tiredness that comes through the slow and prolonged strength drainage of months of toil. There was no power of recuperation left, no reserve strength to call upon. It had been all used, the last least bit of it. Every muscle, every fibre, every cell, was tired, dead tired. And there was reason for it. In less than five months they had travelled twenty-five hundred miles, during the last eighteen hundred of which they had had but five days' rest. When they arrived at Skagway they were apparently on their last legs. They could barely keep the traces taut, and on the down grades just managed to keep out of the way of the sled.

"Mush on, poor sore feets," the driver encouraged them as they tottered down the main street of Skagway. "Dis is de las'. Den we get one long res'. Eh? For sure. One bully long res'."

The drivers confidently expected a long stop-over. Themselves, they had covered twelve hundred miles with two days' rest, and in the nature of reason and common justice they deserved an interval of loafing. But so many were the men who had rushed into the Klondike, and so many were the sweethearts, wives, and kin that had not rushed in, that the congested mail was taking on Alpine proportions;[10] also, there were official orders. Fresh batches of Hudson Bay dogs were to take the places of those worthless for the trail. The worthless ones were to be got rid of, and, since dogs count for little against dollars, they were to be sold.

Three days passed, by which time Buck and his mates found how really tired and weak they were. Then, on the morning of the fourth day, two men from the States came along and bought them, harness and all, for a song. The men addressed each other as "Hal" and "Charles." Charles was a middle-aged, lightish-colored man, with weak and watery eyes and a mustache that twisted fiercely and vigorously up, giving the lie to the limply drooping lip it concealed. Hal was a youngster of nineteen or twenty, with a big Colt's revolver[11] and a hunting-knife strapped about him on a belt that fairly bristled with cartridges. This belt was the most salient thing about him. It advertised his callowness—a callowness sheer and unutterable. Both men were manifestly out of place, and why such as they should adventure the North is part of the mystery of things that passes understanding.

Buck heard the chaffering, saw the money pass between the man and the Government agent, and knew that the Scotch half-breed and the mail-train drivers were passing out of his life on the heels of Perrault and François and the others who had gone before. When driven with his mates to the new owners' camp, Buck saw a slipshod and slovenly affair, tent half stretched, dishes unwashed, everything in disorder; also, he saw a woman. "Mercedes" the men called her. She was Charles's wife and Hal's sister—a nice family party.

Buck watched them apprehensively as they proceeded to take down the tent and load the sled. There was a great deal of effort about their manner, but no businesslike method. The tent was rolled into an awkward bundle three times as large as it should have been. The tin dishes were packed away unwashed. Mercedes continually fluttered in the way of her men and kept up an unbroken chattering of remonstrance and advice. When they put a clothes-sack on the front of the sled, she suggested it should go on the back; and when they had it put on the back, and covered it over with a couple of other bundles, she discovered overlooked articles which could abide nowhere else but in that very sack, and they unloaded again.

Three men from a neighboring tent came out and looked on, grinning and winking at one another.

"You've got a right smart load as it is," said one of them; "and it's not me should tell you your business, but I wouldn't tote that tent along if I was you."

"Undreamed of!" cried Mercedes, throwing up her hands in dainty dismay. "However in the world could I manage without a tent?"

"It's springtime, and you won't get any more cold weather," the man replied.

She shook her head decidedly, and Charles and Hal put the last odds and ends on top the mountainous load.

"Think it'll ride?" one of the men asked.

"Why shouldn't it?" Charles demanded rather shortly.

"Oh, that's all right, that's all right," the man hastened meekly to say. "I was just a-wonderin', that is all. It seemed a mite top-heavy."

Charles turned his back and drew the lashings down as well as he could, which was not in the least well.

"An' of course the dogs can hike along all day with that contraption behind them," affirmed a second of the men.

"Certainly," said Hal, with freezing politeness, taking hold of the gee-pole with one hand and swinging his whip from the other. "Mush!" he shouted. "Mush on there!"

The dogs sprang against the breastbands, strained hard for a few moments, then relaxed. They were unable to move the sled.

"The lazy brutes, I'll show them," he cried, preparing to lash out at them with the whip.

But Mercedes interfered, crying, "Oh, Hal, you mustn't," as she caught hold of the whip and wrenched it from him. "The poor dears! Now you must promise you won't be harsh with them for the rest of the trip, or I won't go a step."

"Precious lot you know about dogs," her brother sneered; "and I wish you'd leave me alone. They're lazy, I tell you, and you've got to whip them to get anything out of them. That's their way. You ask any one. Ask one of those men."

Mercedes looked at them imploringly, untold repugnance at sight of pain written in her pretty face.

"They're weak as water, if you want to know," came the reply from one of the men. "Plumb tuckered out, that's what's the matter. They need a rest."

"Rest be blanked," said Hal, with his beardless lips; and Mercedes said, "Oh!" in pain and sorrow at the oath.

But she was a clannish creature, and rushed at once to the defence of her brother. "Never mind that man," she said pointedly. "You're driving our dogs and you do what you think best with them."

Again Hal's whip fell upon the dogs. They threw themselves against the breastbands, dug their feet into the packed snow, got down low to it, and put forth all their strength. The sled held as though it were an anchor. After two efforts, they stood still, panting. The whip was whistling savagely, when once more Mercedes interfered. She dropped on her knees before Buck, with tears in her eyes, and put her arms around his neck.

"You poor, poor dears," she cried sympathetically, "why don't you pull hard?—then you wouldn't be whipped." Buck did not like her, but he was feeling too miserable to resist her, taking it as part of the day's miserable work.

One of the onlookers, who had been clenching his teeth to suppress hot speech, now spoke up:—

"It's not that I care a whoop what becomes of you, but for the dogs' sakes I just want to tell you, you can help them a mighty lot by breaking out that sled. The runners are froze fast. Throw your weight against the gee-pole, right and left, and break it out."

A third time the attempt was made, but this time, following the advice, Hal broke out the runners which had been frozen to the snow. The overloaded and unwieldy sled forged ahead, Buck and his mates struggling frantically under the rain of blows. A hundred yards ahead the path turned and sloped steeply into the main street. It would have required an experienced man to keep the top-heavy sled upright, and Hal was not such a man. As they swung on the turn the sled went over, spilling half its load through the loose lashings. The dogs never stopped. The lightened sled bounded on its side behind them. They were angry because of the ill treatment they had received and the unjust load. Buck was raging. He broke into a run, the team following his lead. Hal cried, "Whoa! whoa!" but they gave no heed. He tripped and was pulled off his feet. The capsized sled ground over him, and the dogs dashed on up the street, adding to the gayety of Skagway as they scattered the remainder of the outfit along its chief thoroughfare.

Kind-hearted citizens caught the dogs and gathered

up the scattered belongings. Also, they gave advice. Half the load and twice the dogs, if they ever expected to reach Dawson, was what was said. Hal and his sister and brother-in-law listened unwillingly, pitched tent, and overhauled the outfit, canned goods were turned out that made men laugh, for canned goods on the Long Trail is a thing to dream about. "Blankets for a hotel," quoth one of the men who laughed and helped. "Half as many is too much; get rid of them. Throw away that tent, and all those dishes—who's going to wash them anyway? Good Lord, do you think you're travelling on a Pullman?"[12]

And so it went, the inexorable elimination of the superfluous. Mercedes cried when her clothes-bags were dumped on the ground and article after article was thrown out. She cried in general, and she cried in particular over each discarded thing. She clasped hands about knees, rocking back and forth broken-heartedly. She averred she would not go an inch, not for a dozen Charleses. She appealed to everybody and to everything, finally wiping her eyes and proceeding to cast out even articles of apparel that were imperative necessaries. And in her zeal, when she had finished with her own, she attacked the belongings of her men and went through them like a tornado.

This accomplished, the outfit, though cut in half, was still a formidable bulk. Charles and Hal went out in the evening and bought six Outside dogs. These, added to the six of the original team, and Teek and Koona, the huskies obtained at the Rink Rapids on the record trip, brought the team up to fourteen. But the Outside dogs, though practically broken in since their landing, did not amount to much. Three were short-haired pointers, one was a Newfoundland, and the other two were mongrels of indeterminate breed. They did not seem to know anything, these newcomers. Buck and his comrades looked upon them with disgust, and though he speedily taught them their places and what not to do, he could not teach them what to do. They did not take kindly to trace and trail. With the exception of the two mongrels, they were bewildered and spirit-broken by the strange savage environment in which they found themselves and by ill treatment they had received. The two mongrels were without spirit at all; bones were the only things breakable about them.

With the newcomers hopeless and forlorn, and the old team worn out by twenty-five hundred miles of continuous trail, the outlook was anything but bright. The two men, however, were quite cheerful. And they were proud, too. They were doing the thing in style, with fourteen dogs. They had seen other sleds depart over the Pass for Dawson or come in from Dawson, but never had they seen a sled with so many as fourteen dogs. In the nature of Arctic travel there was a reason why fourteen dogs should not drag one sled, and that was that one sled could not carry the food for fourteen dogs. But Charles and Hal did not know this. They had worked the trip out with a pencil, so much to a dog, so many dogs, and so many days, Q. E. D.[13] Mercedes looked over their shoulders and nodded comprehensively, it was all so very simple.

Late next morning Buck led the long team up the

street. There was nothing lively about it, no snap or go in him and his fellows. They were starting dead weary. Four times he had covered the distance between Salt Water and Dawson, and the knowledge that, jaded and tired, he was facing the same trail once more, made him bitter. His heart was not in the work, nor was the heart of any dog. The Outsides were timid and frightened, the Insides without confidence in their masters.

Buck felt vaguely that there was no depending upon these two men and the woman. They did not know how to do anything, and as the days went by it became apparent that they could not learn. They were slack in all things, without order or discipline. It took them half the night to pitch a slovenly camp, and half the morning to break that camp and get the sled loaded in fashion so slovenly that for the rest of the day they were occupied in stopping and rearranging the load. Some days they did not make ten miles. On other days they were unable to get started at all. And on no day did they succeed in making more than half the distance used by the men as a basis in their dog-food computation.

It was inevitable that they should go short on dog-food. But they hastened it by overfeeding, bringing the day nearer when underfeeding would commence. The Outside dogs, whose digestions had not been trained by chronic famine to make the most of little, had voracious appetites. And when, in addition to this, the worn-out huskies pulled weakly, Hal decided that the orthodox ration was too small. He doubled it. And to cap it all, when Mercedes, with tears in her pretty eyes and a quaver in her throat, could not cajole him into giving the dogs still more, she stole from the fish-sacks and fed them slyly. But it was not food that Buck and the huskies needed, but rest. And though they were making poor time, the heavy load they dragged sapped their strength severely.

Then came the underfeeding. Hal awoke one day to the fact that his dog-food was half gone and the distance only quarter covered; further, that for love or money no additional dog-food was to be obtained. So he cut down even the orthodox ration and tried to increase the day's travel. His sister and brother-in-law seconded him; but they were frustrated by their heavy outfit and their own incompetence. It was a simple matter to give the dogs less food; but it was impossible to make the dogs travel faster, while their own inability to get under way earlier in the morning prevented them from travelling longer hours. Not only did they not know how to work dogs, but they did not know how to work themselves.

The first to go was Dub. Poor blundering thief that he was, always getting caught and punished, he had none the less been a faithful worker. His wrenched shoulder-blade, untreated and unrested, went from bad to worse, till finally Hal shot him with the big Colt's revolver. It is a saying of the country that an Outside dog starves to death on the ration of the husky, so the six Outside dogs under Buck could do no less than die on half the ration of the husky. The Newfoundland went first, followed by the three short-haired pointers, the two mongrels hanging more grittily on to life, but going in the end.

By this time all the amenities and gentlenesses of the

Southland had fallen away from the three people. Shorn of its glamour and romance, Arctic travel became to them a reality too harsh for their manhood and womanhood. Mercedes ceased weeping over the dogs, being too occupied with weeping over herself and with quarrelling with her husband and brother. To quarrel was the one thing they were never too weary to do. Their irritability arose out of their misery, increased with it, doubled upon it, outdistanced it. The wonderful patience of the trail which comes to men who toil hard and suffer sore, and remain sweet of speech and kindly, did not come to these two men and the woman. They had no inkling of such a patience. They were stiff and in pain; their muscles ached, their bones ached, their very hearts ached; and because of this they became sharp of speech, and hard words were first on their lips in the morning and last at night.

Charles and Hal wrangled whenever Mercedes gave them a chance. It was the cherished belief of each that he did more than his share of the work, and neither forbore to speak this belief at every opportunity. Sometimes Mercedes sided with her husband, sometimes with her brother. The result was a beautiful and unending family quarrel. Starting from a dispute as to which should chop a few sticks for the fire (a dispute which concerned only Charles and Hal), presently would be lugged in the rest of the family, fathers, mothers, uncles, cousins, people thousands of miles away, and some of them dead. That Hal's view on art, or the sort of society plays his mother's brother wrote, should have anything to do with the chopping of a few sticks of firewood, passes comprehension; nevertheless the quarrel was as likely to tend in that direction as in the direction of Charles's political prejudices. And that Charles's sister's tale-bearing tongue should be relevant to the building of a Yukon fire, was apparent only to Mercedes, who disburdened herself of copious opinions upon that topic, and incidentally upon a few other traits unpleasantly peculiar to her husband's family. In the meantime the fire remained unbuilt, the camp half pitched, and the dogs unfed.

Mercedes nursed a special grievance—the grievance of sex. She was pretty and soft, and had been chivalrously treated all her days. But the present treatment by her husband and brother was everything save chivalrous. It was her custom to be helpless. They complained. Upon which impeachment of what to her was her most essential sex prerogative, she made their lives unendurable. She no longer considered the dogs, and because she was sore and tired, she persisted in riding on the sled. She was pretty and soft, but she weighed one hundred and twenty pounds—a lusty last straw to the load dragged by the weak and starving animals. She rode for days, till they fell in the traces and the sled stood still. Charles and Hal begged her to get off and walk, pleaded with her, entreated, the while she wept and importuned Heaven with a recital of their brutality.

On one occasion they took her off the sled by main strength. They never did it again. She let her legs go limp like a spoiled child, and sat down on the trail. They went on their way, but she did not move. After they had travelled three miles they unloaded the sled, came back for her, and by main strength put her on the sled again.

In the excess of their own misery they were callous to the suffering of their animals. Hal's theory, which he practised on others, was that one must get hardened. He had started out preaching it to his sister and brother-in-law. Failing there, he hammered it into the dogs with a club. At the Five Fingers the dog-food gave out, and a toothless old squaw offered to trade them a few pounds of frozen horse-hide for the Colt's revolver that kept the big hunting-knife company at Hal's hip. A poor substitute for food was this hide, just as it had been stripped from the starved horses of the cattlemen six months back. In its frozen state it was more like strips of galvanized iron, and when a dog wrestled it into his stomach it thawed into thin and innutritious leathery strings and into a mass of short hair, irritating and indigestible.

And through it all Buck staggered along at the head of the team as in a nightmare. He pulled when he could; when he could no longer pull, he fell down and remained down till blows from whip or club drove him to his feet again. All the stiffness and gloss had gone out of his beautiful furry coat. The hair hung down, limp and draggled, or matted with dried blood where Hal's club had bruised him. His muscles had wasted away to knotty strings, and the flesh pads had disappeared, so that each rib and every bone in his frame were outlined cleanly through the loose hide that was wrinkled in folds of emptiness. It was heart-breaking, only Buck's heart was unbreakable. The man in the red sweater had proved that.

As it was with Buck, so was it with his mates. They were perambulating skeletons. There were seven all together, including him. In their very great misery they had become insensible to the bite of the lash or the bruise of the club. The pain of the beating was dull and distant, just as the things their eyes saw and their ears heard seemed dull and distant. They were not half living, or quarter living. They were simply so many bags of bones in which sparks of life fluttered faintly. When a halt was made, they dropped down in the traces like dead dogs, and the spark dimmed and paled and seemed to go out. And when the club or whip fell upon them, the spark fluttered feebly up, and they tottered to their feet and staggered on.

There came a day when Billee, the good-natured, fell and could not rise. Hal had traded off his revolver, so he took the axe and knocked Billee on the head as he lay in the traces, then cut the carcass out of the harness and dragged it to one side. Buck saw, and his mates saw, and they knew that this thing was very close to them. In the next day Koona went, and but five of them remained: Joe, too far gone to be malignant; Pike, crippled and limping, only half conscious and not conscious enough longer to malinger; Sol-leks, the one-eyed, still faithful to the toil of trace and trail, and mournful in that he had so little strength with which to pull; Teek, who had not travelled so far that winter and who was now beaten more than the others because he was fresher; and Buck, still at the head of the team, but no longer enforcing discipline or striving to enforce it, blind with weakness half the time and keeping the trail by the loom of it and by the dim feel of his feet.

It was beautiful spring weather, but neither dogs nor humans were aware of it. Each day the sun rose earlier and set later. It was dawn by three in the morning, and twilight lingered till nine at night. The whole long day was a blaze of sunshine. The ghostly winter silence had given way to the great spring murmur of awakening life. This murmur arose from all the land, fraught with the joy of living. It came from the things that lived and moved again, things which had been as dead and which had not moved during the long months of frost. The sap was rising in the pines. The willows and aspens were bursting out in young buds. Shrubs and vines were putting on fresh garbs of green. Crickets sang in the nights, and in the days all manner of creeping, crawling things rustled forth into the sun. Partridges and woodpeckers were booming and knocking in the forest. Squirrels were chattering, birds singing, and overhead honked the wild-fowl driving up from the South in cunning wedges that split the air.

From every hill slope came the trickle of running water, the music of unseen fountains. All things were thawing, bending, snapping. The Yukon was straining to break loose the ice that bound it down. It ate away from beneath; the sun ate from above. Air-holes formed, fissures sprang and spread apart, while thin sections of ice fell through bodily into the river. And amid all this bursting, rending, throbbing of awakening life, under the blazing sun and through the soft-sighing breezes, like wayfarers to death, staggered the two men, the woman, and the huskies.

With the dogs falling, Mercedes weeping and riding, Hal swearing innocuously, and Charles's eyes wistfully watering, they staggered into John Thornton's camp at the mouth of White River. When they halted, the dogs dropped down as though they had all been struck dead. Mercedes dried her eyes and looked at John Thornton. Charles sat down on a log to rest. He sat down very slowly and painstakingly what of his great stiffness. Hal did the talking. John Thornton was whittling the last touches on an axe-handle he had made from a stick of birch. He whittled and listened, gave monosyllabic replies, and, when it was asked, terse advice. He knew the breed, and he gave his advice in the certainty that it would not be followed.

"They told us up above that the bottom was dropping out of the trail and that the best thing for us to do was to lay over," Hal said in response to Thornton's warning to take no more chances on the rotten ice. "They told us we couldn't make White River, and here we are." This last with a sneering ring of triumph in it.

"And they told you true," John Thornton answered. "The bottom's likely to drop out at any moment. Only fools, with the blind luck of fools, could have made it. I tell you straight, I wouldn't risk my carcass on that ice for all the gold in Alaska."

"That's because you're not a fool, I suppose," said Hal. "All the same, we'll go on to Dawson." He uncoiled his whip. "Get up there, Buck! Hi! Get up there! Mush on!"

Thornton went on whittling. It was idle, he knew, to get between a fool and his folly;[14] while two or three fools more or less would not alter the scheme of things.

But the team did not get up at the command. It had

long since passed into the stage where blows were required to rouse it. The whip flashed out, here and there, on its merciless errands. John Thornton compressed his lips. Sol-leks was the first to crawl to his feet. Teek followed. Joe came next, yelping with pain. Pike made painful efforts. Twice he fell over, when half up, and on the third attempt managed to rise. Buck made no effort. He lay quietly where he had fallen. The lash bit into him again and again, but he neither whined nor struggled. Several times Thornton started, as though to speak, but changed his mind. A moisture came into his eyes, and, as the whipping continued, he arose and walked irresolutely up and down.

This was the first time Buck had failed, in itself a sufficient reason to drive Hal into a rage. He exchanged the whip for the customary club. Buck refused to move under the rain of heavier blows which now fell upon him. Like his mates, he was barely able to get up, but, unlike them, he had made up his mind not to get up. He had a vague feeling of impending doom. This had been strong upon him when he pulled into the bank, and it had not departed from him. What of the thin and rotten ice he had felt under his feet all day, it seemed that he sensed disaster close at hand, out there ahead on the ice where his master was trying to drive him. He refused to stir. So greatly had he suffered, and so far gone was he, that the blows did not hurt much. And as they continued to fall upon him, the spark of life within flickered and went down. It was nearly out. He felt strangely numb. As though from a great distance, he was aware that he was being beaten. The last sensations of pain left him. He no longer felt anything, though very faintly he could hear the impact of the club upon his body. But it was no longer his body, it seemed so far away.

And then, suddenly, without warning, uttering a cry that was inarticulate and more like the cry of an animal, John Thornton sprang upon the man who wielded the club. Hal was hurled backward, as though struck by a falling tree. Mercedes screamed. Charles looked on wistfully, wiped his watery eyes, but did not get up because of his stiffness.

John Thornton stood over Buck, struggling to control himself, too convulsed with rage to speak.

"If you strike that dog again, I'll kill you," he at last managed to say in a choking voice.

"It's my dog," Hal replied, wiping the blood from his mouth as he came back. "Get out of my way, or I'll fix you. I'm going to Dawson."

Thornton stood between him and Buck and evinced no intention of getting out of the way. Hal drew his long hunting-knife. Mercedes screamed, cried, laughed, and manifested the chaotic abandonment of hysteria. Thornton rapped Hal's knuckles with the axe-handle, knocking the knife to the ground. He rapped his knuckles again as he tried to pick it up. Then he stooped, picked it up himself, and with two strokes cut Buck's traces.

Hal had no fight left in him. Besides, his hands were full with his sister, or his arms, rather; while Buck was too near dead to be of further use in hauling the sled. A few minutes later they pulled out from the bank and down the river. Buck heard them go and raised his head

JACK LONDON (1876–1916)

**A GOLD-CRAZED MOB AWAITS
NEWS OF THE LATEST STRIKE**

The outside world did not learn of the gold strike at Bonanza Creek until a steamer arrived in Seattle in 1897 with a shipment of gold from the Klondike. The next year there was a mad rush to the area, and more than 28,000 persons entered the territory. In six months, over five hundred houses had been built in Dawson City.

SLED DOGS STRUGGLING OVER HILLY TERRAIN

Sled dogs became worth almost their weight in gold during the height of the wild rush to the northlands by fortune hunters. A skillful driver, a sturdy sled, and a seasoned team of dogs were indispensable for traveling, delivering mail, or hauling small cargo over the huge expanses of ice and snow that lay between towns.

BUCK, THE YOUNG LORD OF THE ESTATE DOGS

And over this great demesne Buck ruled. Here he was born, and here he had lived the four years of his life. It was true, there were other dogs. There could not be but other dogs on so vast a place, but they did not count. They came and went, resided in the populous kennels, or lived obscurely in the recesses of the house. . . . (page 28)

A SLED DOG IN HARNESS

Before he had recovered from the shock caused by the tragic passing of Curley, he received another shock. François fastened upon him an arrangement of straps and buckles. It was a harness, such as he had seen the grooms put on the horses at home. And as he had seen horses work, so he was set to work. . . . (pages 42–43)

STARVING HUSKIES ATTACK THE TEAM-DOGS

Never had Buck seen such dogs. It seemed as though their bones would burst through their skins. They were mere skeletons, draped loosely in draggled hides, with blazing eyes and slavering fangs. But the hunger-madness made them terrifying, irresistible. There was no opposing them. The team-dogs were swept back against the cliff. . . . (page 55)

THE DEVIL DOG, SPITZ

"One devil, dat Spitz," remarked Perrault. "Some dam day heem keel dat Buck."

"Dat Buck two devils," was François's rejoinder. "All de tam I watch dat Buck I know for sure. Lissen: some dam fine day heem get mad lak hell an' den heem chew dat Spitz all up an' spit heem out on de snow. . . ." (pages 60–61)

DAWSON CITY DURING THE GOLD RUSH

. . . they pulled into Dawson one dreary afternoon. . . . Here were many men, and countless dogs, and Buck found them all at work. It seemed the ordained order of things that dogs should work. All day they swung up and down the main street in long teams, and in the night their jingling bells still went by. (page 63)

FIGHT TO THE DEATH

Every animal was motionless as though turned to stone. Only Spitz quivered and bristled as he staggered back and forth, snarling with horrible menace, as though to frighten off impending death. Then Buck sprang in and out. . . . The dark circle became a dot on the moon-flooded snow as Spitz disappeared from view. (page 70)

INEXPERIENCED PROSPECTORS
"MANIFESTLY OUT OF PLACE"

Charles was a middle-aged, lightish-colored man, with weak and watery eyes and a mustache that twisted fiercely and vigorously up. . . . Hal was a youngster of nineteen or twenty, with a big Colt's revolver and a hunting-knife strapped about him on a belt that fairly bristled with cartridges. This belt . . . advertised his callowness. . . . (pages 84–85)

A TEAM BREAKS THROUGH MELTING ICE

Suddenly, they saw its back end drop down . . . and the gee-pole, with Hal clinging to it, jerk into the air. Mercedes's scream came to their ears. They saw Charles turn and make one step to run back, and then a whole section of ice give way and dogs and humans disappear. A yawning hole was all that was to be seen. (page 101)

THE CALL OF THE WILD

So peremptorily did these shades beckon him, that each day mankind and the claims of mankind slipped farther from him. Deep in the forest a call was sounding, and as often as he heard this call, mysteriously thrilling and luring, he felt compelled to turn his back upon the fire and the beaten earth around it. . . . (page 107)

BONANZA CREEK, SCENE OF
ONE OF THE EARLY BIG GOLD STRIKES

"And break it out? and walk off with it for a hundred yards?"
demanded Matthewson, a Bonanza king....

"And break it out, and walk off with it for a hundred yards,"
John Thornton said coolly.

"Well," Matthewson said, slowly . . . so that all could hear,
"I've got a thousand dollars that says he can't." (page 113)

BUCK WINS A BET FOR THORNTON

The sled swayed and trembled, half-started forward. One of his feet slipped, and one man groaned aloud. Then the sled lurched ahead in what appeared a rapid succession of jerks, though it never really came to a dead stop again . . . half an inch . . . an inch . . . two inches. . . . The jerks perceptibly diminished . . . as the sled gained momentum. . . . (page 118)

PROSPECTORS PANNING FOR GOLD

Spring came on once more, and at the end of all their wandering they found, not the Lost Cabin, but a shallow placer in a broad valley where the gold showed like yellow butter across the bottom of the washing-pan. They sought no farther. Each day they worked earned them thousands of dollars in clean dust and nuggets. . . . (pages 122–123)

AGAIN, THE CALL OF THE WILD

One night he sprang from sleep with a start, eager-eyed, nostrils quivering and scenting, his mane bristling in recurrent waves. From the forest came the call (or one note of it, for the call was many-noted), distinct and definite as never before—a long-drawn howl, like, yet unlike, any noise made by husky dog. (page 125) to see. Pike was leading, Sol-leks was at the wheel, and between were Joe and Teek. They were limping and staggering. Mercedes was riding the loaded sled. Hal guided at the gee-pole, and Charles stumbled along in the rear.

As Buck watched them, Thornton knelt beside him and with rough, kindly hands searched for broken bones. By the time his search had disclosed nothing more than many bruises and a state of terrible starvation, the sled was a quarter of a mile away. Dog and man watched it crawling along over the ice. Suddenly, they saw its back end drop down, as into a rut, and the gee-pole, with Hal clinging to it, jerk into the air. Mercedes's scream came to their ears. They saw Charles turn and make one step to run back, and then a whole section of ice give way and dogs and humans disappear. A yawning hole was all that was to be seen. The bottom had dropped out of the trail.

John Thornton and Buck looked at each other.

"You poor devil," said John Thornton and Buck licked his hand.

6

❧

FOR THE LOVE OF A MAN

New cool
y aund

When John Thornton froze his feet in the previous December, his partners had made him comfortable and left him to get well, going on themselves up the river to get out a raft of saw-logs for Dawson. He was still limping slightly at the time he rescued Buck, but with the continued warm weather even the slight limp left him. And here, lying by the river bank through the long spring days, watching the running water, listening lazily to the songs of birds and the hum of nature, Buck slowly won back his strength.

A rest comes very good after one has travelled three thousand miles, and it must be confessed that Buck waxed lazy as his wounds healed, his muscles swelled out, and the flesh came back to cover his bones. For that matter, they were all loafing—Buck, John Thornton, and Skeet and Nig—waiting for the raft to come that was to carry them down to Dawson. Skeet was a little Irish setter who early made friends with Buck, who in a dying condition, was unable to resent her first advances. She had the doctor trait which some dogs possess, and as a mother cat washes her kittens, so she washed and cleansed Buck's wounds. Regularly, each morning after he had finished his breakfast, she performed her self-appointed task, till he came to look for her ministrations as much as he did for Thornton's. Nig, equally friendly though less demonstrative, was a huge black dog, half bloodhound and half deerhound, with eyes that laughed and a boundless good nature.

To Buck's surprise these dogs manifested no jealousy toward him. They seemed to share the kindliness and largeness of John Thornton. As Buck grew stronger they enticed him into all sorts of ridiculous games, in which Thornton himself could not forbear to join, and in this fashion Buck romped through his convalescence and into a new existence. Love, genuine passionate love, was his for the first time. This he had never experienced at Judge Miller's down in the sun-kissed Santa Clara Valley. With the Judge's sons, hunting and tramping, it had been a working partnership; with the Judge's grandsons, a sort of pompous guardianship; and with the Judge himself, a stately and dignified friendship. But love that was feverish and burning, that was adoration, that was madness, it had taken John Thornton to arouse.

This man had saved his life, which was something; but, further, he was the ideal master. Other men saw to the welfare of their dogs from a sense of duty and business expediency; he saw to the welfare of his as if they were his own children, because he could not help it. And he saw further. He never forgot a kindly greeting or a cheering word, and to sit down for a long talk with them ("gas" he called it) was as much his delight as theirs. He had a way of taking Buck's head roughly between his hands, and resting his own head upon Buck's, of shaking him back and forth, the while calling him ill names that to Buck were love names. Buck knew no greater joy than that rough embrace and the sound of murmured oaths, and at each jerk back and forth it seemed that his heart would be shaken out of his body so great was its ecstasy. And when, released, he sprang to his feet, his mouth laughing, his eyes eloquent, his throat vibrant with unuttered sound, and in that fashion remained without movement, John Thornton would reverently exclaim, "God! you can all but speak!"

Buck had a trick of love expression that was akin to hurt. He would often seize Thornton's hand in his mouth and close so fiercely that the flesh bore the impress of his teeth for some time afterward. And as Buck understood the oaths to be love words, so the man understood this feigned bite for a caress.

For the most part, however, Buck's love was expressed in adoration. While he went wild with happiness when Thornton touched him or spoke to him, he did not seek these tokens. Unlike Skeet, who was wont to shove her nose under Thornton's hand and nudge and nudge till petted, or Nig, who would stalk up and rest his great head on Thornton's knee, Buck was content to adore at a distance. He would lie by the hour, eager, alert, at Thornton's feet, looking up into his face, dwelling upon it, studying it, following with keenest interest each fleeting expression, every movement or change of feature. Or, as chance might have it, he would lie farther away, to the side or rear, watching the outlines of the man and the occasional movements of his body. And often, such was the communion in which they lived, the strength of Buck's gaze would draw John Thornton's head around, and he would return the gaze, without speech, his heart shining out of his eyes as Buck's heart shone out.

For a long time after his rescue, Buck did not like Thornton to get out of his sight. From the moment he left the tent to when he entered it again, Buck would follow at his heels. His transient masters since he had come into the Northland had bred in him a fear that no master could be permanent. He was afraid that Thornton would pass out of his life as Perrault and François and the Scotch half-breed had passed out. Even in the night, in his dreams, he was haunted by this fear. At such times he would shake off sleep and creep through the chill to the flap of the tent, where he would stand and listen to the sound of his master's breathing.

But in spite of this great love he bore John Thornton, which seemed to bespeak the soft civilizing influence, the strain of the primitive, which the Northland had aroused in him, remained alive and active. Faithfulness and devotion, things born of fire and roof, were his; yet he retained his wildness and wiliness. He was a thing of the wild, come in from the wild to sit by John Thornton's fire, rather than a dog of the soft Southland stamped with the marks of generations of civilization. Because of his very great love, he could not steal from this man, but from any other man, in any other camp, he did not hesitate an instant, while the cunning with which he stole enabled him to escape detection.

His face and body were scored by the teeth of many dogs, and he fought as fiercely as ever and more shrewdly. Skeet and Nig were too good-natured for quarrelling—besides, they belonged to John Thornton; but the strange dog, no matter what the breed or valor, swiftly acknowledged Buck's supremacy or found himself struggling for life with a terrible antagonist. And Buck was merciless. He had learned well the law of club and fang, and he never forewent an advantage or drew back from a foe he had started on the way to Death. He had lessoned from Spitz, and from the chief fighting dogs of the police and mail, and knew there was no middle course. He must master or be mastered; while to show mercy was a weakness. Mercy did not exist in the primordial life. It was misunderstood for fear, and such misunderstandings made for death. Kill or be killed, eat or be eaten, was the law; and this mandate, down out of the depths of Time, he obeyed.

He was older than the days he had seen and the breaths he had drawn. He linked the past with the present, and the eternity behind him throbbed through him in a mighty rhythm to which he swayed as the tides and seasons swayed. He sat by John Thornton's fire, a broad-breasted dog, white-fanged and long-furred; but behind him were the shades of all manner of dogs, half-wolves and wild wolves, urgent and prompting, tasting the savor of the meat he ate, thirsting for the water he drank, scenting the wind with him, listening with him and telling him the sounds made by the wild life in the forest, dictating his moods, directing his actions, lying down to sleep with him when he lay down, and dreaming with him and beyond him and becoming themselves the stuff of his dreams.

So peremptorily did these shades beckon him, that each day mankind and the claims of mankind slipped farther from him. Deep in the forest a call was sounding, and as often as he heard this call, mysteriously thrilling and luring, he felt compelled to turn his back upon the fire and the beaten earth around it, and to plunge into the forest, and on and on, he knew not where or why; nor did he wonder where or why, the call sounding imperiously, deep in the forest. But as often as he gained the soft unbroken earth and the green shade, the love for John Thornton drew him back to the fire again.

Thornton alone held him. The rest of mankind was as nothing. Chance travellers might praise or pet him; but he was cold under it all, and from a too demonstrative man he would get up and walk away. When Thornton's partners, Hans and Pete, arrived on the long-expected raft, Buck refused to notice them till he learned they were close to Thornton; after that he tolerated them in a passive sort of way, accepting favors from them as though he favored them by accepting. They were of the same large type as Thornton, living close to the earth, thinking simply and seeing clearly; and ere they swung the raft into the big eddy by the saw-mill at Dawson, they understood Buck and his ways, and did not insist upon an intimacy such as obtained with Skeet and Nig.

For Thornton, however, his love seemed to grow and grow. He alone among men could put a pack upon Buck's back in the summer travelling. Nothing was too great for Buck to do, when Thornton commanded. One day (they had grub-staked themselves from the proceeds of the raft and left Dawson for the head-waters of the Tanana) the men and dogs were sitting on the crest of a cliff which fell away, straight down, to naked bedrock three hundred feet below. John Thornton was sitting near the edge, Buck at his shoulder. A thoughtless whim seized Thornton, and he drew the attention of Hans and Pete to the experiment he had in mind. "Jump, Buck!" he commanded, sweeping his arm out and over the chasm. The next instant he was grappling with Buck on the extreme edge, while Hans and Pete were dragging them back into safety.

"It's uncanny," Pete said, after it was over and they had caught their speech.

Thornton shook his head. "No, it is splendid, and it is terrible, too. Do you know, it sometimes makes me afraid."

"I'm not hankering to be the man that lays hands on you while he's around," Pete announced conclusively, nodding his head toward Buck.

"Py Jingo!" was Hans's contribution. "Not mineself either."

It was at Circle City, ere the year was out, that Pete's apprehensions were realized. "Black" Burton, a man evil-tempered and malicious, had been picking a quarrel with a tenderfoot at the bar, when Thornton stepped good-naturedly between. Buck, as was his custom, was lying in a corner, head on paws, watching his master's every action. Burton struck out, without warning, straight from the shoulder. Thornton was sent spinning, and saved himself from falling only by clutching the rail of the bar.

Those who were looking on heard what was neither bark nor yelp, but a something which is best described as a roar, and they saw Buck's body rise up in the air as he left the floor for Burton's throat. The man saved his life by instinctively throwing out his arm, but was hurled backward to the floor with Buck on top of him. Buck loosed his teeth from the flesh of the arm and drove in again for the throat. This time the man succeeded only in partly blocking, and his throat was torn open. Then the crowd was upon Buck, and he was driven off; but while a surgeon checked the bleeding, he prowled up and down, growling furiously, attempting to rush in, and being forced back by an array of hostile clubs. A "miners' meeting,"[15] called on the spot, decided that the dog had sufficient provocation, and Buck was discharged. But his reputation was made, and from that day his name spread through every camp in Alaska.

Later on, in the fall of the year, he saved John Thornton's life in quite another fashion. The three partners were lining a long and narrow poling-boat down a bad stretch of rapids on the Forty Mile Creek. Hans and Pete moved along the bank, snubbing with a thin manila rope from tree to tree, while Thornton remained in the boat, helping its descent by means of a pole, and shouting directions to the shore. Buck, on the bank, worried and anxious, kept abreast of the boat, his eyes never off his master.

At a particularly bad spot, where a ledge of barely submerged rocks jutted out into the river, Hans cast off the rope, and, while Thornton poled the boat out into the stream, ran down the bank with the end in his hand to snub the boat when it had cleared the ledge. This it did, and was flying down-stream in a current as swift as a mill-race, when Hans checked it with the rope and checked too suddenly. The boat flirted over and snubbed in to the bank bottom up, while Thornton, flung sheer out of it, was carried down-stream toward the worst part of the rapids, a stretch of wild water in which no swimmer could live.

Buck had sprung in on the instant; and at the end of three hundred yards, amid a mad swirl of water, he overhauled Thornton. When he felt him grasp his tail, Buck headed for the bank, swimming with all his splendid strength. But the progress shoreward was slow; the progress down-stream amazingly rapid. From below came the fatal roaring where the wild current went wilder and was rent in shreds and spray by the rocks which thrust through like the teeth of an enormous comb. The suck of the water as it took the beginning of the last steep pitch was frightful, and Thornton knew that the shore was impossible. He scraped furiously over a rock, bruised across a second, and struck a third with crushing force. He clutched its slippery top with both hands, releasing Buck, and above the roar of the churning water shouted: "Go, Buck! Go!"

Buck could not hold his own, and swept on downstream, struggling desperately, but unable to win back. When he heard Thornton's command repeated, he partly reared out of the water, throwing his head high, as though for a last look, then turned obediently toward the bank. He swam powerfully and was dragged ashore by Pete and Hans at the very point where swimming ceased to be possible and destruction began.

They knew that the time a man could cling to a slippery rock in the face of that driving current was a matter of minutes, and they ran as fast as they could up the bank to a point far above where Thornton was hanging on. They attached the line with which they had been snubbing the boat to Buck's neck and shoulders, being careful that it should neither strangle him nor impede his swimming, and launched him into the stream. He struck out boldly, but not straight enough into the stream. He discovered the mistake too late, when Thornton was abreast of him and a bare half-dozen strokes away while he was being carried helplessly past.

Hans promptly snubbed with the rope, as though Buck were a boat. The rope thus tightening on him in the sweep of the current, he was jerked under the surface, and under the surface he remained till his body struck against the bank and he was hauled out. He was half drowned, and Hans and Pete threw themselves upon him, pounding the breath into him and the water out of him. He staggered to his feet and fell down. The faint sound of Thornton's voice came to them, and though they could not make out the words of it, they knew that he was in his extremity. His master's voice acted on Buck like an electric shock. He sprang to his feet and ran up the bank ahead of the men to the point of his previous departure.

Again the rope was attached and he was launched, and again he struck out, but this time straight into the stream. He had miscalculated once, but he would not be guilty of it a second time. Hans paid out the rope, permitting no slack, while Pete kept it clear of coils. Buck held on till he was on a line straight above Thornton; then he turned, and with the speed of an express train headed down upon him. Thornton saw him coming, and, as Buck struck him like a battering ram, with the whole force of the current behind him, he reached up and closed with both arms around the shaggy neck. Hans snubbed the rope around the tree, and Buck and Thornton were jerked under the water. Strangling, suffocating, sometimes one uppermost and sometimes the other, dragging over the jagged bottom, smashing against rocks and snags, they veered in to the bank.

Thornton came to, belly downward and being violently propelled back and forth across a drift log by Hans and Pete. His first glance was for Buck, over whose limp and apparently lifeless body Nig was setting up a howl, while Skeet was licking the wet face and closed eyes. Thornton was himself bruised and battered, and he went carefully over Buck's body, when he had been brought around, finding three broken ribs.

"That settles it," he announced. "We camp right here." And camp they did, till Buck's ribs knitted and he was able to travel.

That winter, at Dawson, Buck performed another exploit, not so heroic, perhaps, but one that put his name many notches higher on the totem-pole of Alaskan fame. This exploit was particularly gratifying to the three men; for they stood in need of the outfit which it furnished, and were enabled to make a long-desired trip into the virgin East, where miners had not yet appeared. It was brought about by a conversation in the Eldorado Saloon,[16] in which men waxed boastful of their favorite dogs. Buck, because of his record, was the target for these men, and Thornton was driven stoutly to defend him. At the end of half an hour one man stated that his dog could start a sled with five hundred pounds and walk off with it; a second bragged six hundred for his dog; and a third, seven hundred.

"Pooh! Pooh!" said John Thornton, "Buck can start a thousand pounds."

"And break it out? and walk off with it for a hundred yards?" demanded Matthewson, a Bonanza king,[17] he of the seven hundred vaunt.

"And break it out, and walk off with it for a hundred yards," John Thornton said coolly.

"Well," Matthewson said, slowly and deliberately, so that all could hear, "I've got a thousand dollars that says he can't. And there it is." So saying, he slammed a sack of gold dust of the size of a bologna sausage down upon the bar.

Nobody spoke. Thornton's bluff, if bluff it was, had

been called. He could feel a flush of warm blood creeping up his face. His tongue had tricked him. He did not know whether Buck could start a thousand pounds. Half a ton! The enormousness of it appalled him. He had great faith in Buck's strength and had often thought him capable of starting such a load; but never, as now, had he faced the possibility of it, the eyes of a dozen men fixed upon him, silent and waiting. Further, he had no thousand dollars; nor had Hans or Pete.

"I've got a sled standing outside now, with twenty fifty-pound sacks of flour on it," Matthewson went on with brutal directness, "so don't let that hinder you."

Thornton did not reply. He did not know what to say. He glanced from face to face in the absent way of a man who has lost the power of thought and is seeking somewhere to find the thing that will start it going again. The face of Jim O'Brien, a Mastodon king and old-time comrade, caught his eyes. It was a cue to him, seeming to rouse him to do what he would never have dreamed of doing.

"Can you lend me a thousand?" he asked, almost in a whisper.

"Sure," answered O'Brien, thumping down a plethoric sack by the side of Matthewson's. "Though it's little faith I'm having, John, that the beast can do the trick."

The Eldorado emptied its occupants into the street to see the test. The tables were deserted, and the dealers and gamekeepers came forth to see the outcome of the wager and to lay odds. Several hundred men, furred and mittened, banked around the sled within easy distance. Matthewson's sled, loaded with a thousand pounds of flour, had been standing for a couple of hours, and in the intense cold (it was sixty below zero) the runners had frozen fast to the hard-packed snow. Men offered odds of two to one that Buck could not budge the sled. A quibble arose concerning the phrase "break out." O'Brien contended it was Thornton's privilege to knock the runners loose, leaving Buck to "break it out" from a dead standstill. Matthewson insisted that the phrase included breaking the runners from the frozen grip of the snow. A majority of the men who had witnessed the making of the bet decided in his favor, whereat the odds went up to three to one against Buck. There were no takers. Not a man believed him capable of the feat. Thornton had been hurried into the wager, heavy with doubt; and now that he looked at the sled itself, the concrete fact, with the regular team of ten dogs curled up in the snow before it, the more impossible the task appeared. Matthewson waxed jubilant.

"Three to one!" he proclaimed. "I'll lay you another thousand at that figure, Thornton. What d'ye say?"

Thornton's doubt was strong in his face, but his fighting spirit was aroused—the fighting spirit that soars above odds, fails to recognize the impossible, and is deaf to all save the clamor for battle. He called Hans and Pete to him. Their sacks were slim, and with his own the three partners could rake together only two hundred dollars. In the ebb of their fortunes, this sum was their total capital; yet they laid it unhesitatingly against Matthewson's six hundred.

The team of ten dogs was unhitched, and Buck, with

his own harness, was put into the sled. He had caught the contagion of the excitement, and he felt that in some way he must do a great thing for John Thornton. Murmurs of admiration at his splendid appearance went up. He was in perfect condition, without an ounce of superfluous flesh, and the one hundred and fifty pounds that he weighed were so many pounds of grit and virility. His furry coat shone with the sheen of silk. Down the neck and across the shoulders, his mane, in repose as it was, half bristled and seemed to lift with every movement, as though excess of vigor made each particular hair alive and active. The great breast and heavy fore legs were no more than in proportion with the rest of the body where the muscles showed in tight rolls underneath the skin. Men felt these muscles and proclaimed them hard as iron, and the odds went down to two to one.

"Gad, sir! Gad, sir!" stuttered a member of the latest dynasty, a king of the Skookum Benches. "I offer you eight hundred for him, sir, before the test, sir; eight hundred just as he stands."

Thornton shook his head and stepped to Buck's side.

"You must stand off from him," Matthewson protested. "Free play and plenty of room."

The crowd fell silent; only could be heard the voices of the gamblers vainly offering two to one. Everybody acknowledged Buck a magnificent animal, but twenty fifty-pound sacks of flour bulked too large in their eyes for them to loosen their pouch-strings.

Thornton knelt down by Buck's side. He took his head in his two hands and rested cheek on cheek. He did not playfully shake him, as was his wont, or murmur soft love curses; but he whispered in his ear. "As you love me, Buck. As you love me," was what he whispered. Buck whined with suppressed eagerness.

The crowd was watching curiously. The affair was growing mysterious. It seemed like a conjuration. As Thornton got to his feet, Buck seized his mittened hand between his jaws, pressing in with his teeth and releasing slowly, half-reluctantly. It was the answer, in terms, not of speech, but of love. Thornton stepped well back.

"Now, Buck," he said.

Buck tightened the traces, then slacked them for a matter of several inches. It was the way he had learned.

"Gee!" Thornton's voice rang out, sharp in the tense silence.

Buck swung to the right, ending the movement in a plunge that took up the slack and with a sudden jerk arrested his one hundred and fifty pounds. The load quivered, and from under the runners arose a crisp crackling.

"Haw!" Thornton commanded.

Buck duplicated the manœuvre, this time to the left. The crackling turned into a snapping, the sled pivoting and the runners slipping and grating several inches to the side. The sled was broken out. Men were holding their breaths, intensely unconscious of the fact.

"Now, MUSH!"

Thornton's command cracked out like a pistol-shot. Buck threw himself forward, tightening the traces with a jarring lunge. His whole body was gathered compactly together in the tremendous effort, the muscles writhing and knotting like live things under the silky fur. His great chest was low to the ground, his head forward and down, while his feet were flying like mad, the claws scarring the hard-packed snow in parallel grooves. The sled swayed and trembled, half-started forward. One of his feet slipped, and one man groaned aloud. Then the sled lurched ahead in what appeared a rapid succession of jerks, though it never really came to a dead stop again . . . half an inch . . . an inch . . . two inches . . . The jerks perceptibly diminished; as the sled gained momentum, he caught them up, till it was moving steadily along.

Men gasped and began to breathe again, unaware that for a moment they had ceased to breathe. Thornton was running behind, encouraging Buck with short, cheery words. The distance had been measured off, and as he neared the pile of firewood which marked the end of the hundred yards, a cheer began to grow and grow, which burst into a roar as he passed the firewood and halted at command. Every man was tearing himself loose, even Matthewson. Hats and mittens were flying in the air. Men were shaking hands, it did not matter with whom, and bubbling over in a general incoherent babel.[18]

But Thornton fell on his knees beside Buck. Head was against head, and he was shaking him back and forth. Those who hurried up heard him cursing Buck, and he cursed him long and fervently, and softly and lovingly.

"Gad, sir! Gad, sir!" spluttered the Skookum Bench king. "I'll give you a thousand for him, sir, a thousand, sir—twelve hundred, sir."

Thornton rose to his feet. His eyes were wet. The tears were streaming frankly down his cheeks. "Sir," he said to the Skookum Bench king, "no, sir. You can go to hell, sir. It's the best I can do for you, sir."

Buck seized Thornton's hand in his teeth. Thornton shook him back and forth. As though animated by a common impulse, the onlookers drew back to a respectful distance, nor were they again indiscreet enough to interrupt.

7

❁

THE SOUNDING OF
THE CALL[19]

When Buck earned sixteen hundred dollars in five minutes for John Thornton, he made it possible for his master to pay off certain debts and to journey with his partners into the East after a fabled lost mine, the history of which was as old as the history of the country. Many men had sought it; few had found it; and more than a few there were who had never returned from the quest. This lost mine was steeped in tragedy and shrouded in mystery. No one knew of the first man. The oldest tradition stopped before it got back to him. From the beginning there had been an ancient and ramshackle cabin. Dying men had sworn to it, and to the mine the site of which it marked, clinching their testimony with nuggets that were unlike any known grade of gold in the Northland.

But no living man had looted this treasure house, and the dead were dead; wherefore John Thornton and Pete and Hans, with Buck and half a dozen other dogs, faced into the East on an unknown trail to achieve where men and dogs as good as themselves had failed. They sledded seventy miles up the Yukon, swung to the left into the Stewart River, passed the Mayo and the McQueston, and held on until the Stewart itself became a streamlet, threading the upstanding peaks which marked the backbone of the continent.

John Thornton asked little of man or nature. He was unafraid of the wild. With a handful of salt and a rifle he could plunge into the wilderness and fare wherever he pleased and as long as he pleased. Being in no haste, Indian fashion, he hunted his dinner in the course of the day's travel; and if he failed to find it, like the Indian, he kept on travelling, secure in the knowledge that sooner or later he would come to it. So, on this great journey into the East, straight meat was the bill of fare, ammunition and tools principally made up the load on the sled, and the time-card was drawn upon the limitless future.

To Buck it was boundless delight, this hunting, fishing, and indefinite wandering through strange places. For weeks at a time they would hold on steadily, day after day; and for weeks upon end they would camp, here and there, the dogs loafing and the men burning holes through frozen muck and gravel and washing countless pans of dirt by the heat of the fire. Sometimes they went hungry, sometimes they feasted riotously, all according to the abundance of game and the fortune of hunting. Summer arrived, and dogs and men packed on their backs, rafted across blue mountain lakes, and descended or ascended unknown rivers in slender boats whipsawed from the standing forest.

The months came and went, and back and forth they twisted through the uncharted vastness, where no men were and yet where men had been if the Lost Cabin were true. They went across divides in summer blizzards, shivered under the midnight sun on naked mountains between the timber line and the eternal snows, dropped into summer valleys amid swarming gnats and flies, and in the shadows of glaciers picked strawberries and flowers as ripe and fair as any the Southland could boast. In the fall of the year they penetrated a weird lake country, sad and silent, where wild-fowl had been, but where then there was no life nor sign of life—only the blowing of chill winds, the forming of ice in sheltered places, and the melancholy rippling of waves on lonely beaches.

And through another winter they wandered on the obliterated trails of men who had gone before. Once, they came upon a path blazed through the forest, an ancient path, and the Lost Cabin seemed very near. But the path began nowhere and ended nowhere, and it remained mystery, as the man who made it and the reason he made it remained mystery. Another time they chanced upon the time-graven wreckage of a hunting lodge, and amid the shreds of rotted blankets John Thornton found a long-barrelled flint-lock. He knew it for a Hudson Bay Company gun of the young days in the Northwest, when such a gun was worth its height in beaver skins packed flat. And that was all—no hint as to the man who in an early day had reared the lodge and left the gun among the blankets.

Spring came on once more, and at the end of all their wandering they found, not the Lost Cabin, but a shallow placer in a broad valley where the gold showed like yellow butter across the bottom of the washing-pan. They sought no farther. Each day they worked earned them thousands of dollars in clean dust and nuggets, and they worked every day. The gold was sacked in moose-hide bags, fifty pounds to the bag, and piled like so much fire-wood outside the spruce-bough lodge. Like giants they toiled, days flashing on the heels of days like dreams as they heaped the treasure up.

There was nothing for the dogs to do save the hauling in of meat now and again that Thornton killed, and Buck spent long hours musing by the fire. The vision of the short-legged hairy man came to him more frequently, now that there was little work to be done; and often, blinking by the fire, Buck wandered with him in that other world which he remembered.

The salient thing of this other world seemed fear. When he watched the hairy man sleeping by the fire, head between his knees and hands clasped above, Buck saw that he slept restlessly, with many starts and awakenings, at which times he would peer fearfully into the darkness and fling more wood upon the fire. Did they walk by the beach of a sea, where the hairy man gathered shell-fish and ate them as he gathered, it was with eyes that roved everywhere for hidden danger and with legs prepared to run like the wind at its first appearance. Through the forest they crept noiselessly, Buck at the hairy man's heels; and they were alert and vigilant, the pair of them, ears twitching and moving and nostrils quivering, for the man heard and smelled as keenly as Buck. The hairy man could spring up into the trees and travel ahead as fast as on the ground, swinging by the arms from limb to limb, sometimes a dozen feet apart, letting go and catching, never falling, never missing his grip. In fact, he seemed as much at home among the trees as on the ground; and Buck had memories of nights of vigil spent beneath trees wherein the hairy man roosted, holding on tightly as he slept.

And closely akin to the visions of the hairy man was the call still sounding in the depths of the forest. It filled him with a great unrest and strange desires. It caused him to feel a vague, sweet gladness, and he was aware of wild yearnings and stirrings for he knew not what. Sometimes he pursued the call into the forest, looking for it as though it were a tangible thing, barking softly or defiantly, as the mood might dictate. He would thrust his nose into the cool wood moss, or into the black soil where long grasses grew, and snort with joy at the fat earth smells; or he would crouch for hours, as if in concealment, behind fungus-covered trunks of fallen trees, wide-eyed and wide-eared to all that moved and sounded about him. It might be, lying thus, that he hoped to surprise this call he could not understand. But he did not know why he did these various things. He was impelled to do them, and did not reason about them at all.

Irresistible impulses seized him. He would be lying in camp, dozing lazily in the heat of the day, when suddenly his head would lift and his ears cock up, intent and listening, and he would spring to his feet and dash away, and on and on, for hours, through the forest aisles and across the open spaces where the niggerheads bunched. He loved to run down dry watercourses, and to creep and spy upon the bird life in the woods. For a day at a time he would lie in the underbrush where he could watch the partridges drumming and strutting up and down. But especially he loved to run in the dim twilight of the summer midnights, listening to the subdued and sleepy murmurs of the forest, reading signs and sounds as man may read a book, and seeking for the mysterious something that called—called, waking or sleeping, at all times, for him to come.

One night he sprang from sleep with a start, eager-eyed, nostrils quivering and scenting, his mane bristling in recurrent waves. From the forest came the call (or one note of it, for the call was many-noted), distinct and definite as never before—a long-drawn howl, like, yet unlike, any noise made by husky dog. And he knew it, in the old familiar way, as a sound heard before. He sprang through the sleeping camp and in swift silence dashed through the woods. As he drew closer to the cry he went more slowly, with caution in every movement, till he came to an open place among the trees, and looking out saw, erect on haunches, with nose pointed to the sky, a long, lean, timber wolf.

He had made no noise, yet it ceased from its howling and tried to sense his presence. Buck stalked into the open, half crouching, body gathered compactly together, tail straight and stiff, feet falling with unwonted care. Every movement advertised commingled threatening and overture of friendliness. It was the menacing truce that marks the meeting of wild beasts that prey. But the wolf fled at sight of him. He followed, with wild leapings, in a frenzy to overtake. He ran him into a blind channel, in the bed of the creek, where a timber jam barred the way. The wolf whirled about, pivoting on his hind legs after the fashion of Joe and of all cornered husky dogs, snarling and bristling, clipping his teeth together in a continuous and rapid succession of snaps.

Buck did not attack, but circled him about and hedged him in with friendly advances. The wolf was suspicious and afraid; for Buck made three of him in weight, while his head barely reached Buck's shoulder. Watching his chance, he darted away, and the chase was resumed. Time and again he was cornered and the thing repeated, though he was in poor condition or Buck could not so easily have overtaken him. He would run till Buck's head was even with his flank, when he would whirl around at bay, only to dash away again at the first opportunity.

But in the end Buck's pertinacity was rewarded; for the wolf, finding that no harm was intended, finally sniffed noses with him. Then they became friendly, and played about in the nervous, half-coy way with which fierce beasts belie their fierceness. After some time of this the wolf started off at an easy lope in a manner that plainly showed he was going somewhere. He made it clear to Buck that he was to come, and they ran side by side through the sombre twilight, straight up the creek bed, into the gorge from which it issued, and across the bleak divide where it took its rise.

On the opposite slope of the watershed they came down into a level country where were great stretches of forest and many streams, and through these great stretches they ran steadily, hour after hour, the sun rising higher and the day growing warmer. Buck was wildly glad. He knew he was at last answering the call, running by the side of his wood brother toward the place from where the call surely came. Old memories were coming upon him fast, and he was stirring to them as of old he stirred to the realities of which they were the shadows. He had done this thing before, somewhere in that other and dimly remembered world, and he was doing it again now, running free in the open, the unpacked earth underfoot, the wide sky overhead.

They stopped by a running stream to drink, and, stopping, Buck remembered John Thornton. He sat down. The wolf started on toward the place from where the call surely came, then returned to him, sniffing noses and making actions as though to encourage him. But Buck turned about and started slowly on the back track. For the better part of an hour the wild brother ran by his side, whining softly. Then he sat down, pointed his nose upward, and howled. It was a mournful howl, and as Buck held steadily on his way he heard it grow faint and fainter until it was lost in the distance.

John Thornton was eating dinner when Buck dashed into camp and sprang upon him, in a frenzy of affection, overturning him, scrambling upon him, licking his face, biting his hand—"playing the general tom-fool," as John Thornton characterized it, the while he shook Buck back and forth and cursed him lovingly.

For two days and nights Buck never left camp, never let Thornton out of his sight. He followed him about at his work, watched him while he ate, saw him into his blankets at night and out of them in the morning. But after two days the call in the forest began to sound more imperiously than ever. Buck's restlessness came back on him, and he was haunted by recollections of the wild brother, and of the smiling land beyond the divide and the run side by side through the wide forest stretches. Once again he took to wandering in the woods, but the wild brother came no more; and though he listened through long vigils, the mournful howl was never raised.

He began to sleep out at night, staying away from camp for days at a time; and once he crossed the divide at the head of the creek and went down into the land of timber and streams. There he wandered for a week, seeking vainly for fresh sign of the wild brother, killing his meat as he travelled and travelling with the long, easy lope that seems never to tire. He fished for salmon in a broad stream that emptied somewhere into the sea, and by this stream he killed a large black bear, blinded by the mosquitoes while likewise fishing, and raging through the forest helpless and terrible. Even so, it was a hard fight, and it aroused the last latent remnants of Buck's ferocity. And two days later, when he returned to his kill and found a dozen wolverenes quarrelling over the spoil, he scattered them like chaff; and those that fled left two behind who would quarrel no more.

The blood-longing became stronger than ever before. He was a killer, a thing that preyed, living on the things that lived, unaided, alone, by virtue of his own strength and prowess, surviving triumphantly in a hostile environment where only the strong survive. Because of all this he became possessed of a great pride in himself, which communicated itself like a contagion to his physical being. It advertised itself in all his movements, was apparent in the play of every muscle, spoke plainly as speech in the way he carried himself, and made his glorious furry coat if anything more glorious. But for the stray brown on his muzzle and above his eyes, and for the splash of white hair that ran midmost down his chest, he might well have been mistaken for a gigantic wolf, larger than the largest of the breed. From his St. Bernard father he had inherited size and weight, but it was his shepherd mother who had given shape to that size and weight. His muzzle was the long wolf muzzle, save that it was larger than the muzzle of any wolf; and his head, somewhat broader, was the wolf head on a massive scale.

His cunning was wolf cunning, and wild cunning; his intelligence, shepherd intelligence and St. Bernard intelligence; and all this, plus an experience gained in the fiercest of schools, made him as formidable a creature as any that roamed the wild. A carnivorous animal, living on a straight meat diet, he was in full flower, at the high tide of his life, overspilling with vigor and virility. When Thornton passed a caressing hand along his back, a snapping and crackling followed the hand, each hair discharging its pent magnetism at the contact. Every part, brain and body, nerve tissue and fibre, was keyed to the most exquisite pitch; and between all the parts there was a perfect equilibrium or adjustment. To sights and sounds and events which required action, he responded with lightning-like rapidity. Quickly as a husky dog could leap to defend from attack or to attack, he could leap twice as quickly. He saw the movement, or heard sound, and responded in less time than another dog required to compass the mere seeing or hearing. He perceived and determined and responded in the same instant. In point of fact the three actions of perceiving, determining, and responding were sequential; but so infinitesimal were the intervals of time between them that they appeared simultaneous. His muscles were surcharged with vitality, and snapped into play sharply, like steel springs. Life streamed through him in splendid flood, glad and rampant, until it seemed that it would burst him asunder in sheer ecstasy and pour forth generously over the world.

"Never was there such a dog," said John Thornton one day, as the partners watched Buck marching out of camp.

"When he was made, the mould was broke," said Pete.

"Py jingo! I t'ink so mineself," Hans affirmed.

They saw him marching out of camp, but they did not see the instant and terrible transformation which took place as soon as he was within the secrecy of the forest. He no longer marched. At once he became a thing of the wild, stealing along softly, cat-footed, a passing shadow that appeared and disappeared among the shadows. He knew how to take advantage of every cover, to crawl on his belly like a snake, and like a snake to leap and strike. He could take a ptarmigan from its nest, kill a rabbit as it slept, and snap in mid air the little chipmunks fleeing a second too late for the trees. Fish, in open pools, were not too quick for him; nor were beaver, mending their dams, too wary. He killed to eat, not from wantonness; but he preferred to eat what he killed himself. So a lurking humor ran through his deeds, and it was his delight to steal upon the squirrels, and, when he all but had them, to let them go, chattering in mortal fear to the tree-tops.

As the fall of the year came on, the moose appeared

in greater abundance, moving slowly down to meet the winter in the lower and less rigorous valleys. Buck had already dragged down a stray part-grown calf; but he wished strongly for larger and more formidable quarry, and he came upon it one day on the divide at the head of the creek. A band of twenty moose had crossed over from the land of streams and timber, and chief among them was a great bull. He was in a savage temper, and, standing over six feet from the ground, was as formidable an antagonist as ever Buck could desire. Back and forth the bull tossed his great palmated antlers, branching to fourteen points and embracing seven feet within the tips. His small eyes burned with a vicious and bitter light, while he roared with fury at sight of Buck.

From the bull's side, just forward of the flank, protruded a feathered arrow-end, which accounted for his savageness. Guided by that instinct which came from the old hunting days of the primordial world, Buck proceeded to cut the bull out from the herd. It was no slight task. He would bark and dance about in front of the bull, just out of reach of the great antlers and of the terrible splay hoofs which could have stamped his life out with a single blow. Unable to turn his back on the fanged danger and go on, the bull would be driven into paroxysms of rage. At such moments he charged Buck, who retreated craftily, luring him on by a simulated inability to escape. But when he was thus separated from his fellows, two or three of the younger bulls would charge back upon Buck and enable the wounded bull to rejoin the herd.

There is a patience of the wild—dogged, tireless,

persistent as life itself—that holds motionless for end-less hours the spider in its web, the snake in its coils, the panther in its ambuscade; this patience belongs pecu-liarly to life when it hunts its living food; and it belonged to Buck as he clung to the flank of the herd, retarding its march, irritating the young bulls, worrying the cows with their half-grown calves, and driving the wounded bull mad with helpless rage. For half a day this contin-ued. Buck multiplied himself, attacking from all sides, enveloping the herd in a whirlwind of menace, cutting out his victim as fast as it could rejoin its mates, wearing out the patience of creatures preyed upon, which is a lesser patience than that of creatures preying.

As the day wore along and the sun dropped to its bed in the northwest (the darkness had come back and the fall nights were six hours long), the young bulls retraced their steps more and more reluctantly to the aid of their beset leader. The down-coming winter was harrying them on to the lower levels, and it seemed they could never shake off this tireless creature that held them back. Besides, it was not the life of the herd, or of the young bulls, that was threatened. The life of only one member was demanded, which was a remoter interest than their lives, and in the end they were content to pay the toll.

As twilight fell the old bull stood with lowered head, watching his mates—the cows he had known, the calves he had fathered, the bulls he had mastered—as they shambled on at a rapid pace through the fading light. He could not follow, for before his nose leaped the mer-ciless fanged terror that would not let him go. Three hundred-weight more than half a ton he weighed; he had lived a long, strong life, full of fight and struggle, and at the end he faced death at the teeth of a creature whose head did not reach beyond his great knuckled knees.

From then on, night and day, Buck never left his prey, never gave it a moment's rest, never permitted it to browse the leaves of trees or the shoots of young birch and willow. Nor did he give the wounded bull opportunity to slake his burning thirst in the slender trickling streams they crossed. Often, in desperation, he burst into long stretches of flight. At such times Buck did not attempt to stay him, but loped easily at his heels, satisfied with the way the game was played, lying down when the moose stood still, attacking him fiercely when he strove to eat or drink.

The great head drooped more and more under its tree of horns, and the shambling trot grew weaker and weaker. He took to standing for long periods, with nose to the ground and dejected ears dropped limply; and Buck found more time in which to get water for himself and in which to rest. At such moments, panting with red lolling tongue and with eyes fixed upon the big bull, it appeared to Buck that a change was coming over the face of things. He could feel a new stir in the land. As the moose were coming into the land, other kinds of life were coming in. Forest and stream and air seemed palpitant with their presence. The news of it was borne in upon him, not by sight or sound, or smell, but by some other and subtler sense. He heard nothing, saw nothing, yet knew that the land was somehow different; that through it strange things were afoot and ranging; and he resolved to investigate after he had finished the business in hand.

At last, at the end of the fourth day, he pulled the great moose down. For a day and a night he remained by the kill, eating and sleeping, turn and turn about. Then, rested, refreshed and strong, he turned his face toward camp and John Thornton. He broke into the long easy lope, and went on, hour after hour, never at loss for the tangled way, heading straight home through strange country with a certitude of direction that put man and his magnetic needle to shame.

As he held on he became more and more conscious of the new stir in the land. There was life abroad in it different from the life which had been there throughout the summer. No longer was this fact borne in upon him in some subtle, mysterious way. The birds talked of it, the squirrels chattered about it, the very breeze whispered of it. Several times he stopped and drew in the fresh morning air in great sniffs, reading a message which made him leap on with greater speed. He was oppressed with a sense of calamity happening, if it were not calamity already happened; and as he crossed the last watershed and dropped down into the valley toward camp, he proceeded with greater caution.

Three miles away he came upon a fresh trail that sent his neck hair rippling and bristling. It led straight toward camp and John Thornton. Buck hurried on, swiftly and stealthily, every nerve straining and tense, alert to the multitudinous details which told a story—all but the end. His nose gave him a varying description of the passage of the life on the heels of which he was travelling. He remarked the pregnant silence of the forest. The bird life had flitted. The squirrels were in hiding. One only he saw,—a sleek gray fellow, flattened against a gray dead limb so that he seemed a part of it, a woody excrescence upon the wood itself.

As Buck slid along with the obscureness of a gliding shadow, his nose was jerked suddenly to the side as though a positive force had gripped and pulled it. He followed the new scent into a thicket and found Nig. He was lying on his side, dead where he had dragged himself, an arrow protruding, head and feathers, from either side of his body.

A hundred yards farther on, Buck came upon one of the sled-dogs Thornton had bought in Dawson. This dog was thrashing about in a death-struggle, directly on the trail, and Buck passed around him without stopping. From the camp came the faint sound of many voices, rising and falling in a sing-song chant. Bellying forward to the edge of the clearing, he found Hans, lying on his face, feathered with arrows like a porcupine. At the same instant Buck peered out where the spruce-bough lodge had been and saw what made his hair leap straight up on his neck and shoulders. A gust of overpowering rage swept over him. He did not know that he growled, but he growled aloud with a terrible ferocity. For the last time in his life he allowed passion to usurp cunning and reason, and it was because of his great love for John Thornton that he lost his head.

The Yeehats were dancing about the wreckage of the spruce-bough lodge when they heard a fearful

roaring and saw rushing upon them an animal the like
of which they had never seen before. It was Buck, a
live hurricane of fury, hurling himself upon them in a
frenzy to destroy. He sprang at the foremost man (it
was the chief of the Yeehats), ripping the throat wide
open till the rent jugular spouted a fountain of blood.
He did not pause to worry the victim, but ripped in
passing, with the next bound tearing wide the throat of
a second man. There was no withstanding him. He
plunged about in their very midst, tearing, rending,
destroying, in constant and terrific motion which defied the arrows they discharged at him. In fact, so in-
conceivably rapid were his movements, and so closely
were the Indians tangled together, that they shot one
another with the arrows; and one young hunter, hurling a spear at Buck in mid air, drove it through the
chest of another hunter with such force that the point
broke through the skin of the back and stood out beyond. Then a panic seized the Yeehats, and they fled in
terror to the woods, proclaiming as they fled the ad-
vent of the Evil Spirit.

And truly Buck was the Fiend incarnate, raging at
their heels and dragging them down like deer as they
raced through the trees. It was a fateful day for the Yeehats. They scattered far and wide over the country, and
it was not till a week later that the last of the survivors
gathered together in a lower valley and counted their
losses. As for Buck, wearying of the pursuit, he returned
to the desolated camp. He found Pete where he had
been killed in his blankets in the first moment of surprise. Thornton's desperate struggle was fresh-written

on the earth, and Buck scented every detail of it down to the edge of a deep pool. By the edge, head and fore feet in the water, lay Skeet, faithful to the last. The pool itself, muddy and discolored from the sluice boxes, effectually hid what it contained, and it contained John Thornton; for Buck followed his trace into the water, from which no trace led away.

All day Buck brooded by the pool or roamed restlessly above the camp. Death, as a cessation of movement, as a passing out and away from the lives of the living, he knew, and he knew John Thornton was dead. It left a great void in him, somewhat akin to hunger, but a void which ached and ached, and which food could not fill. At times, when he paused to contemplate the carcasses of the Yeehats, he forgot the pain of it; and at such times he was aware of a great pride in himself—a pride greater than any he had yet experienced. He had killed man, the noblest game of all, and he had killed in the face of the law of club and fang. He sniffed the bodies curiously. They had died so easily. It was harder to kill a husky dog than them. They were no match at all, were it not for their arrows and spears and clubs. Thenceforward he would be unafraid of them except when they bore in their hands their arrows, spears, and clubs.

Night came on, and a full moon rose high over the trees into the sky, lighting the land till it lay bathed in ghostly day. And with the coming of the night, brooding and mourning by the pool, Buck became alive to a stirring of the new life in the forest other than that which the Yeehats had made. He stood up, listening and scenting. From far away drifted a faint, sharp yelp, followed by a chorus of similar sharp yelps. As the moments passed the yelps grew closer and louder. Again Buck knew them as things heard in that other world which persisted in his memory. He walked to the centre of the open space and listened. It was the call, the many-noted call, sounding more luringly and compelling than ever before. And as never before, he was ready to obey. John Thornton was dead. The last tie was broken. Man and the claims of man no longer bound him.

Hunting their living meat, as the Yeehats were hunting it, on the flanks of the migrating moose, the wolf pack had at last crossed over from the land of streams and timber and invaded Buck's valley. Into the clearing where the moonlight streamed, they poured in a silvery flood; and in the centre of the clearing stood Buck, motionless as a statue, waiting their coming. They were awed, so still and large he stood, and a moment's pause fell, till the boldest one leaped straight for him. Like a flash Buck struck, breaking the neck. Then he stood, without movement, as before, the stricken wolf rolling in agony behind him. Three others tried it in sharp succession; and one after the other they drew back, streaming blood from slashed throats or shoulders.

This was sufficient to fling the whole pack forward, pell-mell, crowded together, blocked and confused by its eagerness to pull down the prey. Buck's marvellous quickness and agility stood him in good stead. Pivoting on his hind legs, and snapping and gashing, he was everywhere at once, presenting a front which was apparently unbroken so swiftly did he whirl and guard

from side to side. But to prevent them from getting behind him, he was forced back, down past the pool and
into a creek bed, till he brought up against a high gravel
bank. He worked along to a right angle in the bank
which the men had made in the course of mining, and in
this angle he came to bay, protected on three sides and
with nothing to do but face the front.

And so well did he face it, that at the end of half an
hour the wolves drew back discomfited. The tongues of
all were out and lolling, the white fangs showing cruelly
white in the moonlight. Some were lying down with
heads raised and ears pricked forward; others stood on
their feet, watching him; and still others were lapping
water from the pool. One wolf, long and lean and gray,
advanced cautiously, in a friendly manner, and Buck
recognized the wild brother with whom he had run for a
night and a day. He was whining softly, and, as Buck
whined, they touched noses.

Then an old wolf, gaunt and battle-scarred, came forward. Buck writhed his lips into the preliminary of a
snarl, but sniffed noses with him. Whereupon the old
wolf sat down, pointed nose at the moon, and broke out
the long wolf howl. The others sat down and howled.
And now the call came to Buck in unmistakable accents.
He, too, sat down and howled. This over, he came out of
his angle and the pack crowded around him, sniffing in
half-friendly, half-savage manner. The leaders lifted the
yelp of the pack and sprang away into the woods. The
wolves swung in behind, yelping in chorus. And Buck
ran with them, side by side with the wild brother, yelping as he ran.

And here may well end the story of Buck. The years were not many when the Yeehats noted a change in the breed of timber wolves; for some were seen with splashes of brown on head and muzzle, and with a rift of white centering down the chest. But more remarkable than this, the Yeehats tell of a Ghost Dog that runs at the head of the pack. They are afraid of this Ghost Dog, for it has cunning greater than they, stealing from their camps in fierce winters, robbing their traps, slaying their dogs, and defying their bravest hunters.

Nay, the tale grows worse. Hunters there are who fail to return to the camp, and hunters there have been whom their tribesmen found with throats slashed cruelly open and with wolf prints about them in the snow greater than the prints of any wolf. Each fall, when the Yeehats follow the movement of the moose, there is a certain valley which they never enter. And women there are who become sad when the word goes over the fire of how the Evil Spirit came to select that valley for an abiding-place.

In the summers there is one visitor, however, to that valley, of which the Yeehats do not know. It is a great, gloriously coated wolf, like, and yet unlike, all other wolves. He crosses alone from the smiling timber land and comes down into an open space among the trees. Here a yellow stream flows from rotted moose-hide sacks and sinks into the ground, with long grasses growing through it and vegetable mould overrunning it and hiding its yellow from the sun; and here he muses for a time, howling once, long and mournfully, ere he departs.

But he is not always alone. When the long winter

nights come on and the wolves follow their meat into the lower valleys, he may be seen running at the head of the pack through the pale moonlight or glimmering borealis, leaping gigantic above his fellows, his great throat a-bellow as he sings a song of the younger world, which is the song of the pack.

BIOGRAPHICAL BACKGROUND

———————— ❧ ————————

A critic once remarked of Jack London, "The greatest story he ever wrote was the story he lived." His short, turbulent life was filled with the brutal realities that are found in the dreams of many romantic-minded young-sters. And his tales reflect the harsh truths that underlie each fantastic narrative adventure.

Born in San Francisco on January 12, 1876, the son of William Chaney and Flora Wellman (who later mar-ried John London), young "Jack," as he persisted in call-ing himself despite schoolteachers and editors, grew up in the comparatively underprivileged home of an unsuc-cessful truck gardener. Life was hard, but the boy found escape through his growing interest in reading. He was particularly fascinated by stories featuring the "rags to riches" theme and high adventure.

When the family fortune declined even further and the Londons moved to Oakland, Jack was only ten, but for him the scramble for a living became a stark neces-sity. He delivered papers, did odd jobs on weekends, and began to look upon school as an increasing chore—

although his passion for reading was stronger than ever. At the age of fourteen, he quit school and soon found himself putting in long, backbreaking hours in a cannery. But factory life was not for him, and before long he set out to search, as most boys do only in daydreams, for the thrills of adventure.

Having heard wild tales from an opium smuggler and a harpooner whom he had met a few years earlier, Jack borrowed money, bought the sloop *Razzle Dazzle,* and, at sixteen, became a pirate. He prowled the San Francisco Bay in his boat, robbing the oyster beds and consorting with all manner of villainous characters. And yet, with typical contradictory whim, the following year he worked with the harbor police to suppress just such pirating. This strange attitude, at one moment lawless and reckless, the next law-abiding and civilized, is the major conflict that London's animal and human heroes face time after time.

When he was seventeen, Jack once again heard the call of something wilder and enlisted as a sailor on a sealing expedition, visiting ports as far away as Siberia and Japan. Upon his return, he continued to gratify his restless spirit. He joined the San Francisco affiliates of "Coxey's Army," spent a year as a tramp, and subsequently served a term as a vagrant. Finally, Jack temporarily had his fill of adventure and earnestly returned to high school.

Having completed his secondary education, young London spent a year at the University of California. Unfortunately, partly through lack of funds, partly because he was dissatisfied with the quality of instruction he was receiving in writing, and perhaps again because of his own insatiable wanderlust, he left college and, in 1897, went off to the Klondike in quest of gold. The rest is literary history, for his trip to Canada and Alaska, although winning him no riches, provided him with enough writing materials for a lifetime. He now had his major literary locale—the northern wilderness, the life of Indians, campers, trappers, prospectors, and animals.

During the next seventeen years, London published close to fifty books, and it is not difficult to find reasons for his tremendous success at home and abroad. Younger readers took to his tales because of their spirit of high adventure and suspense, their glorification of courage and personal prowess in overcoming physical perils, and their stress on brutal conflict. We might shudder at the frequent descriptions of violent struggles to a bloody death, but their fascination cannot be denied.

For a more mature audience, London seemed a fresh breeze in the stale Victorian air of much in American fiction. His contempt for false culture reflected the unspoken disappointment of much of the general public in seeing a rugged America too fast withdrawing behind the genteel parlor curtains. He awoke in his readers the early pioneer's awareness of man's direct relations with the natural elements and the raw combat for physical survival.

Even the most sophisticated and discerning readers of London's day found, over and above his romantic wrappings, a prize package of serious ideas. London had managed to dramatize very convincingly the principles of evolution and the law of natural selection that Charles Darwin had described in his *Origin of Species*. Moreover, London's interest in the laboring class and the effectiveness of group action by depressed masses prompted him to flirt with the ideas of Karl Marx. And the use of the concept of a "superman" (or his animal counterpart in Buck), who depends solely upon his own "will to power," delivered the astonishing and dangerous theories of Friedrich Nietzsche into the hands of a superb storyteller.

Perhaps the ease with which London could translate difficult biological, economic, and philosophical ideas into startling fiction is a measure of him as an artist and as a man. Full of whims and furies, never totally committed to anything, he seemed to delight in dramatizing only the most shocking aspects of life and thought. To emphasize his own contempt for flabby idealism, London once said, "Morality is only an evidence of low blood pressure."

Thus, his life and his art were filled with striking contradictions. London was a wealthy capitalist who toyed with socialism, a supreme egotist who fought for the expression of the common man, a preacher of equality who worshiped at the shrine of power. Winning and losing fortunes, participating in two unhappy marriages, feeling himself fallen far short of his unrealistic goals, Jack London died under mysterious circumstances on November 22, 1916, after what was publicly known as a long illness.

HISTORICAL BACKGROUND

As this country headed for the twentieth century, the United States was in the grip of a severe depression that had struck shortly after Grover Cleveland's second inauguration in 1893. A great squabble over currency arose, and the Populist party, the most successful third party in our history, was demanding the coinage of silver at a ratio of 16 to 1. William Jennings Bryan caught the fancy of the Democrats with his famous "Cross of Gold" speech and was nominated for the presidency in 1896 to run against his Republican opponent, William McKinley, who held out stoutly for the gold standard and was elected.

The historical background for *The Call of the Wild* can be limited to the great Klondike gold strike in northwest Canada. The resultant mad rush for easy riches created a great demand for sled dogs, and this need was indirectly responsible for Buck's illegal sale by Manuel. Had not the bootlegging of likely looking animals become a profitable business, Judge Miller's pet might have lived out his days in the California sunshine instead of being kidnaped for shipment to the mining areas.

The first claim in the Klondike was staked out by a prospector, Robert Henderson, in 1895. Sharing the secret was George W. Carmack, who made a huge strike on August 17, 1896, along Bonanza Creek (see reference to Matthewson: p. 113). Then the panic was on. The gold fever gripped men in all parts of the world, and soon the Canadian and later the Alaskan wilds became meccas for get-rich-quick adventurers.

Cities like Juneau and Skagway sprang up seemingly overnight as the need for lodgings, food, and supplies grew. It is said that more than five hundred homes were built in less than six months in Dawson City alone, and within a year this town became the center of one of the richest mining districts in the world.

With the exception of a few who struck it rich, life for the prospectors was not the romantic adventure it had promised before they set out. For every story of a man who returned to San Francisco after a few weeks of mining with $150,000, there were hundreds of tragic tales of death and disease on the trail. As was indicated before, Jack London returned empty-handed, too, except that at least he discovered a great treasure in his mind and pen.

It was not easy to endure the hardships created by the Klondike climate. Winter, with temperatures quite casually falling to fifty degrees below zero, reigns supreme for seven months of the year. The landscape is virtually bare of vegetation, although ample fish and game are to be found. During the spring months and into the summer, from about May 15 to August 7, this is the "Land of the Midnight Sun," with daylight being practically continuous. For the miners, recreation consisted mainly of gambling, carousing, and fighting in the numerous saloons that mushroomed all over the territory as siphons to drain off the hard-won gold dust from the unwary or lonely prospector. With so much excitement and wild spending going on as routines of the day, it is no wonder that writers like London found an endless supply of material for the stories that told of heroic deeds by man and beast or dastardly crimes solved by equally heroic Northwest Mounted Police, the lawmen of the Yukon.

This was the savage, ruthless world into which Buck was thrust, snatched from the warmth of a peaceful fireside and kindly human companionship. That he survived, and even prospered, is the great tribute London pays to this magnificent animal.

LITERARY ALLUSIONS
AND NOTES

1. **Chinese lottery:** The importation of Chinese laborers into the West for the building of the railroads introduced a number of gambling games like "Chinese lottery" and the card game of fan tan.

2. **hydrophoby:** Hydrophobia (from the Latin for "fear of water"), caused by the bite of a rabid animal, is a dread disease. See the references to it p. 57 and p. 60. The kidnaper, uneducated, gets the word a little wrong, a fact which helps to characterize him.

3. **the goose hang high:** In English, we have a number of old sayings and proverbs concerned with geese: "All his geese are swans," "Don't kill the goose that lays the golden egg," "What's sauce for the goose is sauce for the gander," and so on. The expression "The goose hangs high" means "All is well."

4. **the lesson was driven home to Buck:** To some extent, the whole novel is the education of the dog. Here, he learns that "a man with a club was a law-giver,

a master to be obeyed." Later, he will learn to fear no man who is without a weapon. On p. 42, he learns something else: "So that was the way. No fair play. Once down, that was the end of you." On p. 95, he discovers that "one must get hardened." On p. 106, it is: "Kill or be killed, eat or be eaten."

5. **dam bully dog:** Perrault, the French-Canadian who speaks a broken English—*sacredam* is half-French, half-bowdlerized English for "holy damn"—seems to have picked up Theodore Roosevelt's favorite slang word, *bully* (meaning "very good"). The word originated in England in the seventeenth century, was transported to "the Colonies," and by mid-nineteenth century meant "crack" or "first-rate."

6. **"T'ree vair' good dogs":** Like many writers (Eugene O'Neill among them), London had a tin ear and rendered dialect badly. Perrault, the government courier, should be speaking the language of the French Canadians faithfully rendered into phonetic English, but for this, one has to go to Canadian writers such as William Henry Drummond. In London's novel, Perrault can sometimes pronounce *th* (an English sound difficult for speakers of a number of European languages) and sometimes cannot: and the author is not much more reliable in rendering the speech of other nationalities: see p. 108 (for Hans's dialect) and the "stage Irish" of O'Brien (p. 114).

7. **Buck was afterward to learn:** London's use of foreshadowing of events is a literary device as old as the

Greeks (who called it *prolepsis*). It creates suspense and helps to propel the story onward.

8. **Northwest Police:** The Northwest Mounted Police were organized in 1873 to bring law and order to Canada's Northwest Territories, and are better known as the red-coated Mounties of the RCMP (Royal Canadian Mounted Police, to which the name was changed in 1920). They and the Hudson's Bay Company outposts—we encounter "Hudson Bay dogs" on p. 84 and a "Hudson Bay Company gun" (p. 122)— were representatives of civilization and trade in the early days of the frozen North. As early as 1670, "Gentleman Adventurers trading into Hudson's Bay" were chartered by the English king Charles II to encourage exploration and trade and were given a valuable monopoly. The Hudson's Bay Company was reorganized into a stock company in 1863 and forced to sell its territories to Canada for £300,000 in 1869, two years after confederation created the Dominion of Canada. In London's time, the HBC was no longer a fur-trading monopoly but a vast corporation under its active governor, Lord Strathcona. London's story, of course, allows him to touch only lightly on the RCMP and the HBC, but they add dimension and color to his tale of "the Arctic darkness."

9. **not the faintest whisper of air:** In *Modern Painters* (1856) the critic John Ruskin invented the phrase "pathetic fallacy" to describe the literary device of attributing to natural objects and animals human capacities and feelings. Here the very air seems to hold its

breath, like the dogs in an "expectant circle," to await the outcome of the great struggle.

10. **Alpine proportions:** London's way of saying the mail was piling up. The Alps, of course, are mountains.

11. **Colt's revolver:** Now we would say "a Colt." London's way of saying it, here and elsewhere in his story, places the writing of the novel closer than we are to Samuel Colt (1814–1862), the inventor of a revolving-breech pistol, whose surname was eventually established as a generic name for a revolver. Here we see some evidence of the American language in its constant state of flux. Likewise (pp. 86 and 87), in expressions like "a-wonderin'," "a mite top-heavy," "contraption," "Plumb tuckered out," we hear the accents of an earlier time, in this case, the common speech of uneducated pioneers, backwoodsmen, and farmers drawn to Skagway by the lure of gold.

12. **Pullman:** George Mortimer Pullman (1831–1897) was a cabinet-maker who in 1859 converted some railway carriages to be more comfortable for long train journeys and five years later created the first sleeping coach, *The Pioneer.* Of course the stalwart pioneers in Skagway regard these fairly new-fangled inventions with contempt. They are used to far rougher travel accommodations and associate Pullman cars with "tenderfeet."

13. **Q.E.D.:** The Latin *"quod erat demonstrandum"* ("which was to be proved") traditionally appeared as

"Q.E.D." at the end of mathematical proofs, and its use here implies that the "tenderfeet" think of the trip as a problem to be solved neatly and easily, ignoring the human element and their own inexperience. As it turns out, it was not "so very simple" after all, and the reader receives a hint of the disastrous outcome to be expected.

14. **get between a fool and his folly:** Thornton is wise in the ways of the world, and this bit of proverbial wisdom is characteristic. A fool and his money are soon parted, but a fool and his folly are inseparable, thinks Thornton—which relieves him of responsibility for trying to avert the disaster, which he accepts (as so many of us do in connection with other people's disasters) with equanimity. Apparently, civilized people lack the "primordial" instincts (as London continually calls them) that even "dumb animals" enjoy.

15. **"miners' meeting":** Rough justice in the mining camps and boomtowns of the West and the Far North was meted out in kangaroo courts and "miners' meetings," informal town councils. They led as often to lynchings as to acquittals.

16. **Eldorado Saloon:** The name of the saloon is appropriate, recalling as it does the legend of vast riches and *el dorado* (the fabled gold country the Spanish conquistadors sought). The story was that the Chibcha Indians (Colombia, South America) each year anointed their chief with some sticky substance and rolled him in gold dust. Pizarro and Orellana explored

the Amazon (as did Federmann, Benalcázar, and Quesada in Venezuela and New Granada) in search of fabled riches. Sir Walter Raleigh and Coronado also quested in vain for El Dorado.

17. **Bonanza king:** The "Bonanza king," Mastodon (p. 114), and Skookum Benches (p. 116) mines—created by the gold strikes—were the royalty of the gold-rush frontier, having made men who had "struck it rich" immensely wealthy. These men became the leaders and inspirations of all those who sought for a claim that would "pan out," a "mother lode" that would give birth to a vast fortune. They were, says London, the founders of dynasties of wealth. They built palaces to live in and whole booming towns, which disappeared when there was no more precious metal to be mined.

18. **babel:** This is a reference to the biblical story of the descendants of Noah who, in their pride, undertook to erect a tower that would reach Heaven. God frustrated their efforts by miraculously causing the workmen to speak languages unintelligible to each other, from which we get the words *babel* and *babble,* suggesting incomprehensible speech.

19. **The Sounding of the Call** (chapter title): On p. 107 we read: "Deep in the forest a call was sounding," and now we have a chapter devoted to just what that call was. For the man, it was the call of adventure, the lure of riches, the siren call of the lost mine. For the dog, it was an equally compelling drive: "a

great unrest and strange desires" (p. 124). The working out of these two themes constitutes the gripping conclusion of the tale, the culmination of the stories of man and beast that are intertwined in *The Call of the Wild*.

CRITICAL EXCERPTS

❦

1. I call an animal, a species, an individual corrupt, when it loses its instincts, when it chooses, when it prefers, what is injurious to it. (Nietzsche, *The Antichrist,* VI, 1888)

2. If this youthful California writer makes a study of literary style, it is not apparent, so simply and unaffectedly does he relate a story. There is, indeed, small showing of that painstaking polish so dear to the academic mind: this young man of twenty-four has something more virile to offer than finish. Crude as is his diction, he has learned the ways out of prescribed literature into a spontaneity and freedom that charm and invigorate. One sees no straining after effect, no circumlocution; he reaches the humanity of his readers by direct course. (Winetta Fames, *Overland Monthly,* May 1900)

[It was the success of his early stories in the *Overland Monthly* and *The Black Cat* that encouraged London to become a full-time writer.]

3. Form or subject that he happens to choose to write in or about matters little. It is the same vivid, virile personality pouring itself out in a wealth of words that mean warmth and strength or pitiless cold and pitiless cruelty—extreme in either case; exaggerated, but alive, always alive. This is Jack London, and it is of very little importance whether he is writing a story about a man or a dog, about a wolf or a whaler; whether he gives us a sociological treatise on the city slums or a love story in letters. We enjoy it all because it is Jack London, not because it is whatever it happens to be in outer form. (Grace I. Colbron, *Bookman,* February 1907)

4. In *The Call of the Wild* (1903) he made his first distinct impression upon a wide public. London pictured in a great dog, mixture of St. Bernard and shepherd, a response to the primitive call of the wolf pack from which he had originally come. The love of Buck, the dog, for John Thornton, who saves him from an ignorant master who was driving his dogs beyond endurance, is quite natural. But London endows Buck with human qualities which no dog has shown. For example, "He linked the past with the present, and the eternity behind him throbbed through him in a mighty rhythm to which he swayed as the tides and seasons swayed." The best scenes are those in which Buck fights for the supremacy of the pack, or in which he revenges himself upon the Yeehat Indians who have killed Thornton. Here Buck follows his instincts. But in the description of the dog's motives, London is often absurd. What made the book attractive was the direct, forcible style,

the celebration of primitive force, and the new setting of the Alaskan gold fields. (Arthur Hobson Quinn, *American Fiction: An Historical and Critical Survey*, Appleton-Century-Crofts, Inc., 1936)

5. For thirty glorious, labor-laden days he wrote with his thick pencil on the rough scratch paper, made his few word corrections, and transferred the material to the typewriter. He neglected everything else—friends, family, debts, the new baby, galley proof arriving in daily batches from Macmillan; living only with his dog Buck. . . .

Then at a Wednesday open house Jack made good his neglect of his friends. He settled himself in the comfortable lounging chair by the fire while his guests placed themselves in the window seats and on cushions on the floor. With a grave look in his gray-blue eyes, one hand combing fondly through his hair, he read to them the story of the great dog Buck, who remained faithful to his love of man until the call of the forest and the recollection of wild wolves drew him back to primitive life. There were no card games that night, no wild laughter or practical jokes. Jack read until one in the morning, the silence growing ever deeper about him. When he had finished, his usually loquacious friends could say little, but he saw their thoughts in their shining eyes. His three years of writing Alaskan tales had been at last justified; he had expressed himself in an art form so flawlessly and completely that for these few hours his listeners shared with him the ecstasy he had known in its creation. (Irving Stone, *Jack London, Sailor on Horseback*, Houghton Mifflin, 1938)

6. Ordinarily one takes a febrile over-excitement and love of excessive violence to be signs of weakness; but in Jack London they were not—he really did have strength. So likewise in his writing: his fury of language and intemperance of emotion have led some critics to deny that he possesses genuine vigor and power. But to do so is surely an error; those who are not too offended by his excesses can hardly fail to feel his force. Only, in his books as in his own life and character, the strength he had is turned, as if he could realize it only in fighting, coercion, and destruction, not to creation, but to violence. (T. K. Whipple, *Saturday Review*, September 1938)

7. I would rather be ashes than dust! I would rather that my spark should burn out in a brilliant blaze than that it should be stifled by dry-rot. I would rather be a superb meteor, every atom of me in magnificent glow, than a sleepy, and permanent planet. The proper function of man is to live, not to exist. I shall not waste my days in trying to prolong them. I shall use my time. (Jack London, quoted by Joan London in *Jack London and His Times*, 1939)

8. *The Call of the Wild,* summary as well as summit of London's achievement, is the story of a dog stolen from civilization to draw a sledge in Alaska, eventually to escape from human control and go back to the wild as leader of a pack of wolves. As in most animal tales the narrative is sentimentalized. Buck has a psychology which he derives too obviously from his human creator; learns the law of the brute wilderness too quickly and too consciously; dreams too definitely of the savage

progenitors from whom he inherits, by way of atavism, his ability to contend with a new world. This sympathetic fallacy, however, has behind it a reality in London's own experience which lends power to the drama of Buck's restoration to the primitive. In something of this fashion the young tramp had learned the hard rules of the road; in something of this fashion the gold-seeker had mastered the difficulties of the Klondike face to face with a nature which made no allowance for his handicaps and which apparently desired the destruction of the men who had ventured into the wilderness. Out of his experience he had built up a doctrine concerning the essential life of mankind, and out of his doctrine he had shaped this characteristic tale. But the doctrine is not excessively in evidence, and the experience contributes both an accurate lore and an authentic passion. The narrative is as spare as an expedition over the Chilkoot Pass; it is swift and strong, packed with excitement and peril. Moreover, it has what almost none of Jack London's red blood rivals had, and what he later deprived himself of by his haste and casualness: a fine sensitiveness to landscape and environment, a robust, moving, genuine current of poetry which warms his style and heightens the effect while enriching it. It is perhaps his exciting story rather than his explicit doctrines which made him one of the most popular proletarian writers in the world. (Carl Van Doren, *The American Novel 1789–1939*, The Macmillan Company, 1940)

9. He remains one of America's most significant writers because he concerned himself with the vital problems

of his age. Of working class origin, he was the first American writer to portray his class sympathetically and one of the few to use literature for building the foundations of a future society. He was not educated in the formal sense, but his comprehension was so great that he rose above educated men in ability and power to portray in his writings the fundamental issues of our times. The spirit of the common people of America, heroic, fiery, and adventurous will live forever in the pages of his rebel stories, novels, and essays. (Philip S. Foner, *Jack London, American Rebel,* The Citadel Press, 1947)

[This estimate ignores Stephen Crane and Frank Norris—whom London's daughter Joan in her book *Jack London and His Times* (1939) links with him as "the three young pioneers who at the turn of the century had blazed the literary trails into modern American literature"—and a number of other writers who portray the working class with insight and sympathy.]

10. In a number of his novels London found better, though never thoroughly convincing symbols to contain his longing for reversion to the primitive. *The Call of the Wild* (1903), his first successful book and in most respects his masterpiece, is the story of a huge dog which escapes from an Alaskan dog-team to join a wolf-pack. Though Buck carries with him a good many human faculties which no animal could conceivably possess, he serves well enough as a poetic dream-image by means of which the author can express his joy in sheer muscular power and brute ferocity. The narrative moves through a succession of exciting adventures of the ro-

bust and red-blooded kind that perhaps contributed as much as anything else to London's popular appeal. (Arthur Hobson Quinn, ed., *The Literature of the American People: An Historical and Critical Survey*, Appleton-Century-Crofts, Inc., 1951)

11. I think part of the reason for London's popularity in Europe is that he is a very intense writer at his best, and the great élan and vigor that are properly associated with this country and its people emerge often from his pages. To a Europe drained dry of such faculties, it is understandable that London's people, their concerns and their virtues, should have a nostalgic appeal, that Europeans might even read of them as other more credulous generations read of such heroic figures as Roland and Hector. (Harry Sylvester, *The New York Times*, August 19, 1951)

12. Writing to Jack London was never more than a means to an end, and the end was material advancement. "In a certain sense," Joan London observes shrewdly, "this attitude was typically working class. . . ." He wrote his thousand words a day, and when they were done he was finished. He never skipped a day because the spirit failed him, and apparently he was never caught up by his daemon and carried beyond the daily stint. He professed, indeed, to hate writing, and in his last years he was frankly cynical and unpainstaking about it; it was because he had betrayed his art that his art, at last, failed to save him from the forces that were destroying him.

The most important single literary influence upon

him was probably that of Kipling. He valued "strength of utterance" above "precision of utterance," and in so far as he had a literary creed it was to have his characters tell the story by deeds and utterance, eliminating the author as much as possible. His style, characteristically simple and free-flowing, can be eloquent; sometimes it is repetitive and clumsy; it is hardly ever carefully wrought.

Perhaps London came closest to complete success in *White Fang* and *The Call of the Wild*. Theodore Roosevelt's accusation of nature-faking must be at least partially sustained, and if nature-faking is a greater fault here than in "Krazy Kat" or "The Nun's Priest's Tale," the reason is simply that London's books set up certain claims in the way of scientific accuracy that the other works never made. These two stories are, nevertheless, eloquent, impassioned, and spontaneous; they represent a daring and successful use of the imagination. And though the "red in tooth and claw" aspect is somewhat overplayed, it must be admitted that this is nicely overbalanced by the account of Scott's conquest of White Fang through love.

What place in American literature will finally be assigned to Jack London, it is still, more than a generation after his death, somewhat difficult to say. His daughter calls him "last of the writers to celebrate the American frontier, first to trumpet the battles on the frontier of social justice." Though neither her "first" nor her "last" is accurate, the statement is still very suggestive. His materials and his beliefs were more naturalistic than his art. As Professor Pattee has observed, he seems realistic when he is writing about a life that we do not know, but he is much less convincing when he gets upon our own ground. He wrote of "the stress and strain of life, its fevers and sweats and wild indulgences" as a lovesick boy writes about his sweetheart; he made a romance of savagery. (Edward Wagenknecht, *Cavalcade of the American Novel*, Henry Holt and Company, 1952)

13. A subhuman world of instinctual emotion and, in its purest expression, of complete animal identification was the one in which he moved so easily and so instinctively himself. And the dominant mood was of primitive fear or, at its best, of brief and still terror-haunted and transient pleasure amidst all the horrors of the jungle. (Maxwell Geismar, *Rebels and Ancestors*, Houghton Mifflin Company, 1953)

14. London's instinct was to feel life as chaos and battle and to exult in the strength which produced both, but his intelligence, which was not of the most acute, tried to rationalize instinct, to fit jagged pieces into a design, and so he found laws operating in the vast spaces of the far North: the law of natural selection, the law of Eskimo and Indian whereby iron sank in water and women obeyed men, and the law of the white man, enforced by stalwart Mounted Police. Since London's eye was not single, since he could not decide whether he was a disciple of Nietzsche or of Marx, he compromised a narrative gift originally distinguished by vigor, freshness, and dramatic proficiency, and eventually wrote some of the poorest novels of the day. (Grant C. Knight, *The Strenuous Age in American Literature*, The University of North Carolina Press, 1954)

15. At twenty-one he set out for the Klondike where, in 1897, the gold-rush recalled the days of the forty-niners.

On his return voyage Jack London began to plan the stories that presently made him famous as the "Kipling of the Klondike," though he wrote later of other scenes and many other types. Mexican prize-fighters, Chinese, Hawaiians, and what not. In his Alaskan stories he sounded the note of the "strenuous life" that Roosevelt had struck in a speech one year before him, the theme that life is a struggle for survival in a world that is cruel and grim but in which the fighting will has a chance to triumph. In the title story of *The Son of the Wolf* the daughter of an Indian chief in the North is captured, in the teeth of her suitors, by a white lover, and most of the stories, with their Kiplingesque swagger, abounded in scenes of violent death and the conflict of man with the "white silence" and the savagery of nature. This second, wilder Bret Harte world of miners' cabins, bars and flats, of Russian fur-traders, Eskimos, half-breeds and squawmen, was the last corner of the Western frontier that bordered on a wilderness where only the caribou and the wolf were able to survive. One felt that Jack London's stories had been somehow lived,—that the author was not telling tales but telling his life.

In later stories, long or short, *The Call of the Wild, The Faith of Men, A Daughter of the Snows, Children of the Frost,* Jack London continued to recreate this world of the long arctic night in which men fought with men and with hunger and cold. (Van Wyck Brooks and Otto L. Bettmann, *Our Literary Heritage: A Pictorial His-*

tory of the Writer in America, E. P. Dutton & Company, Inc., 1956)

16. From childhood London had had a devouring interest in books: now, he set himself, with unflagging, dynamic energy, to the task of becoming an author. In 1900 his first volume, a group of Alaskan adventure stories, was published. In 1903 appeared his masterpiece, *The Call of the Wild,* in which he illustrated, in an Alaskan setting, the biological trait of atavism—that is, the reappearance in an animal of the instincts and habits of its remote ancestors. The civilized dog, Buck, after being stolen from a luxurious home in southern California, is sent to the savage environment of the Far North, there to struggle for survival under the law of club and fang. As Buck fights his way to leadership among the sleigh-dogs, wild, predatory traits of his ancestors, always latent within him, are awakened and when his master, John Thornton, is killed, he abandons the last trace of human civilization to become the leader of a wolf pack.

Such a primitive story, in the atmosphere of decadence and over-civilization which enveloped the turn-of-the-century years, came to its readers as a bracing wind. Page after page, as they found, is filled with genuine adventure—Perrault and François struggling over all but impossible trails, Buck and Spitz battling to the death for leadership, John Thornton being rescued from the rapids. Page after page throbs with responsiveness to the pale, savage beauty of the Far North—snow trails and frozen lakes, swift rivers, forests of fir, long nights with the aurora borealis flashing coldly across the sky. And on page after page, London's vision of beauty and of brutal adventure forms itself into a strong, rhythmical, semi-poetic style which more than anything else lifts *The Call of the Wild* from the level of mere entertainment to that of true literature.

The philosophy of *The Call of the Wild* consists in a glorification of sheer strength and cunning. London's hero is—insofar as human traits can be attributed to a dog—a savage individualist, exulting with the strength of the strong in the struggle for existence, fighting his way to mastery with the ruthlessness of the dominant primordial brute. Doubtless London felt an instinctive sympathy with these traits in human nature. (Walter Fuller Taylor, *The Story of American Letters*, Henry Regnery Company, 1956)

17. The world was still knee-deep in Victorian morals, traditions, and ideals when Jack London burst upon the literary scene. To the generations exposed to the sentimental pap of the popular writers of the day, his stories of savage realism and heroic conflict had the effect of a tidal wave, sweeping before them the false, romantic idealism that was the vogue. The world as he saw it (as reflected in his writings) was hostile and cruel, with only the brave and the strong having any chance for survival. He refused to shrink from life's unpleasant and brutal side, yet his work retained more than a good measure of romanticism. He bridged the gap between the nineteenth and twentieth centuries and blazed the trail for a new, more realistic school of writing. . . .

The passage of almost half a century has had little effect on the dramatic, forceful, unique character of Jack London's work; it retains its ability to enthrall, excite, and entertain. He remains one of the most successful writers in the history of American letters. As recently as 1952, as a result of a worldwide survey, the United Nations agency Unesco reported that Jack London was the most popular, most widely translated American author in Europe, Russia, and the Iron Curtain countries. (Irving Shepard, Introduction, *Jack London's Tales of Adventure*, Hanover House, 1956)

18. The kind of man who survives and leads is the blond beast, the superman for whom a mate equally scornful of convention usually waits in the next chapter. Sometimes his admirable brutishness sleeps beneath a veneer of civilization and has to be wakened. London's notion of reversion to the primitive is an interesting variation on the naturalistic idea of devolution, for to London it is a wholly admirable transformation. The dog who becomes a wolf in *The Call of the Wild* (1903) is still London's most popular hero.* Socialist though he professed to be, London believed that the mass of men must be ruled by the few—because "most men are fools, and therefore must be taken care of by the few men who are wise." The "few" who were fit to rule were inevitably Anglo-Saxons.

Such was the "inexorable, blind, unreasoning" law which London professed to believe. Actually he com-

---

*London was fond of the word *wolf*. He used to sign his letters "Wolf." The word turns up in titles to his stories, and the ranch house he built at the end of his life was called "Wolf House."

promised most of the time with the conventional morality of his age. (Willard Thorp, *American Writing in the
Twentieth Century*, Harvard University Press, 1960)

19. The background is a cruel Alaska winter; among
the many human characters are Buck's master [John
Thornton], grief at whose death makes the dog take to the
wilds, and other prospectors of the Klondike Gold Rush.
London works out in the course of the story ideas on the
need for adaptation to survive and on the influence of
heredity. The book is at once sentimental and poetic.
(Max Herzberg et al., *Reader's Encyclopedia of American
Literature*, Thomas Y. Crowell Company, 1962)

20. The two dog stories, *The Call of the Wild* (1903)
and *White Fang* (1906), are more successful because
they are uncomplicated by the problem of sex in society.
The love of dog and man may be studied in primitive
terms more readily than may that of man and woman.
In the one book a dog breaks with the codes of civilization and reverts, step by step, to its wolf origins; in the
other a part-wolf is gradually weaned from the wild and
takes his place in the world of his man-god. *The Call of
the Wild* is London's most satisfying work. The theme
and action are in tune, the character of Buck is fully realized, the story proceeds with the economy and sure
strokes of a writer in full command of his material. But
never again, except in occasional short stories where the
task is easier because less ambitious, did he so sharpen
his focus and so completely realize his biological thesis
in fictional form. (Spiller et al., eds., *Literary History of
the United States*, The Macmillan Company, 1963)

21. Jack London's stories still compel the reader to read on. He learned to tell a tale, he says, when he was bumming across the United States and had to decide exactly the right story to pitch in the moment between the housewife opening the door and her asking what he wanted. A slip-up meant no food, perhaps even having the dog set on him. He tells his stories like a tramp. At the end you are left with no distillation of truth, no new vision of life. But you have experienced something vicariously; frozen to death in the Yukon, knocked senseless in the prize-ring, tossed by storm in the Pacific. (Arthur Calder-Marshall, Introduction, *The Bodley Head Jack London*, The Bodley Head, 1963)

22. He survives today chiefly as a storyteller with a vigor and freshness that carries over, with a recurring sense of discovery, to each new generation of readers. Undoubtedly that appeal will increase. In the appallingly overcrowded world predicted for the near future, his vivid word-pictures of empty seascapes and uncluttered lands, and of the free and self-reliant individuals who contended with them and each other, will be a breath of fresh air from the simpler past. No one excelled him as a reporter-participant on the retreating remnants of our frontiers. As a self-made intellectual, he will be interesting only as a curiosity, as an example of the social ferment in the early part of the century. His Socialism shrivels into absurdity against the searing light of Soviet reality. (Richard O'Connor, *Jack London*, Little, Brown and Company, 1964)

23. In spite of his belief in collectivism as an inevitable next step in human evolution, London was most convincing in his depiction of individualistic struggle and primitive violence. The very titles of many of his books, e.g. *The Strength of the Strong* (1911) and *The Abysmal Brute* (1913), indicate his preoccupation with the concept of the brute which underlies the social behavior of men and animals. Buck, in *The Call of the Wild*, shows a retrogression, while *White Fang* [1906] and *Jerry of the Islands* [1917, Jerry is an Irish setter puppy in the South Seas] depict the brute under control or in process of subjugation. Wolf Larsen [ruthless captain in *The Sea Wolf*, 1904] is a combination of civilized brain with primitive force. In *The Iron Heel*, one of the most impressive scenes shows the people of the abyss fighting with bestial, reckless fury against their oppressors. London worshipped Marx and Nietzsche impartially, grasping what he could of their diametrically opposed theories, and championing now one, now the other, both in his novels and in his own life. (James D. Hart, *The Oxford Companion to American Literature*, Oxford University Press, 1965)

24. London was at the height of his powers in 1902 when he began writing the dog story which he thought of as balancing his account of the vicious husky given in "Bâtard." London finished *The Call of the Wild* in just over a month, his prose flowing pure and sharp with the story line, free from excessive exposition of intellectual theory. . . .

The story ends with a sentence that shows London at

his best, a sentence that must have flowed in triumph from a writer who had come to the end of his purest book. . . .

At first glance *The Call of the Wild* seems to be entirely outside any traditional society and therefore far from its tensions, but in fact the narrative reveals various sorts of relations to the patterns of such a society. The values of love and fair play are central to the story; these are traditional and even heroic values. . . . These are presented as atavistic, but they are also "moral" qualities that have always been respected in Western literature. (Charles Child Walcutt, *Jack London,* University of Minnesota Pamphlets on American Writers Number 57, University of Minnesota Press, 1966)

25. In 1896 gold was found in the Klondike; the "gold fever" of the miners who had opened California in 1849 broke out again, in Alaska. Jack London packed his grub and trekked over the Chilkoot Pass, seeking fame and fortune. He struck no gold, but he did find a rich lode in literature, for he wrote *Call of the Wild*. This swashbuckling tale appealed to the armchair adventurers who had stayed behind in their comfortable lives but who liked to entertain dreams of hardship and heroism. The book was the bestseller of 1903, one of the best of the 51 books London wrote over 16 years. (L. R. N. Ashley, *Other People's Lives: 34 Short Stories,* Houghton Mifflin Company, 1970)

26. *The Call of the Wild* can no more be dismissed as a dog story than *Moby-Dick* can be dismissed as a whale story. Indeed, Alfred Kazin's fine insight—that

Melville's Ishmael "sees the whale's view of things," that
he speaks for the primordial, transhuman world of nature—can equally well be applied to London. Both
Melville and London attain a kind of double vision,
sensing the alien character of the natural world while at
the same time feeling a deep kinship with it. This is not
a matter of observing, as some critics have done, that
the dog story involves a human "allegory," a term imply-
ing that Buck is merely a human being disguised as a
dog. Rather, the intuition at the heart of the novel is that
the processes of individuation in a dog, a wolf, or a
human child are not fundamentally different. Somehow,
out of the dim memories of his own childhood, London
recaptures the groping steps by which the very young
deal with the mystifying sensations of their world, learning that snow is cold and fluffy, that fire burns, that
some people are kind and others cruel. This is the "primordial vision" that Earle Labor has rightly insisted is a
distinctive facet of London's imagination. (Charles N.
Watson, Jr., *The Novels of Jack London: A Reappraisal*,
University of Wisconsin Press, 1983)

27. During his long sickness Jack London wrote two of
his major novels, *The Call of the Wild* and *The Sea-Wolf*.
Both books delve into London's past, but the first book
loses itself in the "womb of time," while the second resolutely takes the story into the bright light of the present. . . . *The Call of the Wild* came out of that black abyss
into which London had sunk after his experiences in the
East End of London. . . . *The Call of the Wild* is a lyric not
to what is possible or logical but to what the heart desires.

The book is, indeed, mysteriously moving. Through Buck, his dog hero, London was able to release emotions he perhaps did not know he harbored. . . . Written just after his vision of the urban jungle and its city savages, this book conveys London's revulsion from modern life as it expressed itself in this escape to the "howling and naked savagery" of a wilderness jungle. At the same time that this was an escape, it was also, paradoxically, a return. Upon completion of *The People of the Abyss*, London had consciously closed the book on his working-class past. That self dwelt in a black and slippery pit to be recalled only in dreams. But in *The Call of the Wild* London was able, through his canine hero, to return to the scenes of his past, and, having got in touch with them, to imagine a different future. (Joan D. Hedrick, *Solitary Comrade*, University of North Carolina Press, 1986)

28. London began writing *The Call of the Wild*, the book that would one day make him famous, as a 4,000-word companion to an earlier dog story, "Bâtard." However, within a two-month span (1 December 1902 through January 1903), London had completed a 27,000-word novel. As he explained in a letter to his editor, George P. Brett, "The whole history of this story has been very rapid. On my return from England I sat down to write it into a 4,000 word yarn, but it got away from me & I was forced to expand it to its present length." Macmillan snapped up the rights to the book for $2,000 cash, and the American serial rights were sold to the *Saturday Evening Post* for 3¢ a word, bring-

ing in an additional $750, which London received on 3 March. This was probably the worst deal London made in his life, for the copyrights alone for this book, which sold by the ten millions of copies around the world, would have solved many of the financial problems that plagued his life. But he had really no idea that he had written a world's best-seller and classic, and he merely expected that Macmillan would get a "fair sale" out of it. (Jacqueline Tavernier-Courbin, *"The Call of the Wild":* *A Naturalistic Romance*, Twayne, 1994)

29. But it is *The Call of the Wild*'s very resistance to transparent allegory that is remarkable insofar as we continue to imagine London's hero as a dog despite all his complex mental attributes. London's surprise at his contemporaries' assessment of his tale as an allegorical treatment of the human jungle may very well have been feigned. Yet the fact remains that he does manage to make Buck look and act like a dog-hero until the very end of his narrative, even if at times Buck's nature as a beast needs to be reinforced by simile. When we read at one point that Buck enters camp so exhausted that he "lay down like a dead dog," we are forced to make a dizzying series of negotiations that prevent us from resting easily in either human or animal realms.

How does London manage this effect? First, Buck is powerfully gendered in ways that cut across species lines, so that his maleness allows London to hold onto the animal as a "he." Second—and more complex—is the pattern London sets up in the first half of the narrative whereby Buck is put into a situation not under his control and invested with a human mentality and morality to evaluate the situation, to give it *values* that coincide with London's own as narrator; he is then represented as reacting to that situation by way of "instinct." This black-box biological explanation enables London to maintain the doctrinaire survival-of-the-fittest logic that ostensibly drives his plot. (Jonathan Auerbach, *Male Call*, Duke University Press, 1996)

30. Buck's initiation, his response to a call "to mature selfhood and triumphant life," as Charles N. Watson, Jr., aptly puts it, is also a homecoming. His heeding of this call is a return not so much through time as out of time, to a prehistory of perfect harmony with nature. He edges away from John Thornton's campfire toward the Younger World of the hairy man, and finally touches noses with the Wild Brother, who is certainly a long-submerged level of himself. Successfully crossing the threshold, severing ties with civilization after John Thornton's death, he enters the Abiding Place—that particularly resonant term London used here, I believe, for the first time. There Buck is subsumed into myth and becomes the Ghost Dog, father of a new tribe.

Buck's is the most convincing success story in London's fiction—indeed, one could argue, in the entire tradition of American masculine literature. Looking back along that tradition and viewing the pairs of male characters—Natty and Chingachgook, Ishmael and Queequeg, Huck and Jim—we see that London has sensed and clarified its underlying logic. Those bondings of white males and supposedly primitive sidekicks represented a desire to recover an element of self, a lost harmony with nature and instinct, a condition recalled in dream and in myth. (Charles L. Crow, "Ishi and London's Primitives," in *Rereading Jack London*, edited by Leonard Cassuto and Jeanne Campbell Reesman, Stanford University Press, 1996)

31. London misinformed readers about animal behavior in *The Call of the Wild*. Buck, returning to the spoils of a kill, finds a dozen wolverines, among nature's most vicious creatures. "He scattered them like chaff; and those that fled left two behind who would quarrel no more." (London used *wolves* and *wolverines* interchangeably in his stories, not realizing that vicious wolverines would have slaughtered White Fang.) Buck also beats an entire wolf pack. . . . As Theodore Roosevelt reasoned: "The modern 'nature faker' is of course an object of derision to every scientist worthy of the name, to every real lover of the wilderness, to every faunal naturalist, to every true hunter or nature lover. But it is evident that he completely deceives many good people who are wholly ignorant of wild life. Sometimes he draws on his own imagination for his fictions; sometimes he gets them second-hand from irresponsible guides or trappers or Indians." (John Perry, *Jack London: An American Myth*, Nelson-Hall, 1981, in Katie de Koster, ed., *Readings on "The Call of the Wild,"* The Greenhaven Press, 1999)

32. *The Call of the Wild* and *The Sea-Wolf* are his masterpieces. Of these not a great deal may be said that

is not repetitive. *The Call of the Wild* is the greatest dog-story ever written and is at the same time a study of one of the most curious and profound motives that plays hide-and-seek in the human soul. The more civilized we become the deeper is the fear that back in barbarism is something of the beauty and joy of life we have not brought along with us. We all feel these artificialities that so easily cramp and fret our lives. But this sense of a too-extreme complexity of life, too many tailors, launderers and chefs, too many walls and ceilings that shut out the stars, too many carpets lacking the odor of green grass or the tang of crisp snow, it is this sense you can't educate or civilize out of man. It is in all of us. Not the rankest degenerate but vaguely feels this call back to "nature and his primal sanities," the call of the wild. That the race is soon ripe for new and saner modes of life is shown in the widespread reception of *The Call of the Wild*. The book appeals to people of red blood and clear eyes and the way I have seen boys and girls and old men and hacked-up literary connoisseurs take to this book, makes my heart beat high for the final destiny of the human mob. (Charles A. Sandburg, "Jack London: A Common Man," *Tomorrow* Magazine, 2 April 1906, in Jeanne Campbell Reesman, *Jack London*, Twayne Publishers, 1999)

SUGGESTIONS FOR
FURTHER READING

❦

Auerbach, Jonathan. *Male Call: Becoming Jack London.* Durham, NC: Duke University Press, 1996.

Cassuto, Leonard, and Jeanne Campbell Reesman, eds. *Rereading Jack London.* Stanford, CA: Stanford University Press, 1996.

de Koster, Katie, ed. *Readings on "The Call of the Wild."* San Diego: The Greenhaven Press, 1999.

Dirst Johnson, Claudia, ed. *Understanding "The Call of the Wild": A Student Casebook to Issues, Sources, and Historical Documents.* Westport, CT: Greenwood Press, 2000.

Foner, Philip S. *Jack London, American Rebel.* New York: Citadel Press, 1947.

Freeman, A. W. *A Search for Jack London.* Chicago: Adams Press, 1973.

Hamilton, David Mike. *"Tools of My Trade": The Annotated Books in Jack London's Library.* Seattle: University of Washington Press, 1986.

Hedrick, Joan D. *Solitary Comrade: Jack London and His Work.* Chapel Hill, NC: University of North Carolina Press, 1982.

Hendricks, King. *Jack London: Master Craftsman of the Short Story.* Logan, UT: Utah State University Press, 1966.

Johnston, Carolyn. *Jack London: An American Radical?* Westport, CT: Greenwood Press, 1984.

Kershaw, Alex. *Jack London, A Life*. New York: St. Martin's Press, 1997.

Kingman, Russ. *A Pictorial Life of Jack London*. New York: Crown Publishers, 1979.

Labor, Earle. *Jack London*. New York: Twayne Publishers, 1974.

———— and Jeanne Campbell Reesman. *Jack London*, rev. ed. New York: Twayne Publishers, 1994.

London, Joan. *Jack London and His Times: An Unconventional Biography*. New York: The Book League of America, 1939.

Lundquist, James. *Jack London: Adventures, Ideas, and Fiction*. New York: Ungar, 1988.

Martin, Stoddard. *California Writers: Jack London, John Steinbeck, The Tough Guys*. New York: St. Martin's Press, 1983.

McClintock, James. *Jack London's Strong Truths: A Study of His Short Stories*. East Lansing, MI: Michigan State University Press, 1975.

Nuernberg, Susan, ed. *The Critical Response to Jack London*. Westwood, CT: Greenwood Press, 1995.

O'Conner, Richard. *Jack London: A Biography*. Boston: Little, Brown, 1964.

Ownbey, Ray Wilson. *Jack London: Essays in Criticism*. Santa Barbara, CA: Peregrine Smith, 1978.

Perry, John. *Jack London: An American Myth*. Chicago: Nelson-Hall, 1981.

Reesman, Jeanne Campbell. *Jack London: A Study of the Short Fiction*. New York: Twayne Publishers, 1999.

Sherman, Joan. *Jack London: A Reference Guide*. Boston: G. K. Hall, 1977.

Sinclair, Andrew. *Jack: A Biography of Jack London*. New York: Harper and Row, 1977.

Stone, Irving. *Jack London, Sailor on Horseback*. New York: Houghton Mifflin, 1938.

Tavernier-Courbin, Jacqueline. *"The Call of the Wild": A Naturalistic Romance*. New York: Twayne Publishers, 1994.

————, ed. *Critical Essays on Jack London*. Boston: G. K. Hall, 1983.

Walker, Dale L., and James E. Sisson III. *The Fiction of Jack London: A Chronological Bibliography*. El Paso: Texas Western Press, 1972.

Walker, Franklin Dickerson. *Jack London and the Klondike: The Genesis of an American Writer*. San Marino, CA: Huntington Library, 1966.

Watson, Charles N., Jr. *The Novels of Jack London: A Reappraisal*. Madison, WI: University of Wisconsin Press, 1983.